AF432150

Also by Evan A. Cushing

Fiction:

FANG Net

The Time Hunter Tales:

Mind Wanderer
The Lost Finders
Knight of the Wolves
Storm from the Past
New Tales of the Old World
The Heroic Calamity

Poetry:

Pathfinding

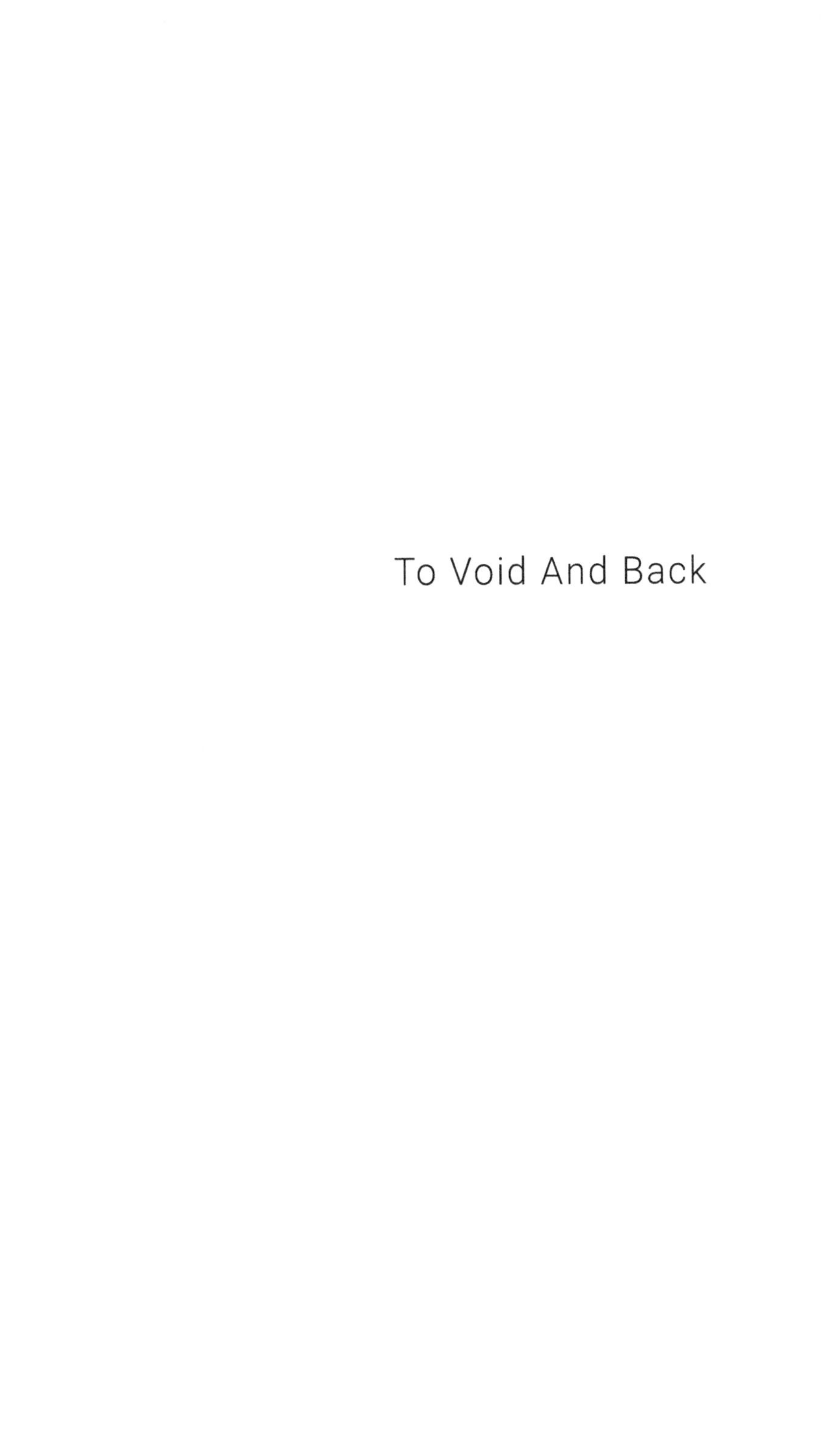

To Void And Back

To Void And Back

Evan A. Cushing

To Void And Back

Published by Primordial Albion Press, 6 Albion Street, Salem, MA, USA

ISBN: 979-8-9873278-4-5 (paperback)
         979-8-9873278-5-2 (eBook)
Library of Congress Control Number: 2026905161

CONTENTS

Prologue: To Begin Again

Lindy sat in her realm of Death. It had been around a thousand years, as mortals understood it, since Lindy had become one of an infinite number of Deaths.

Lindy watched over five worlds in her vast white room, where 5001 desks were set up, populated by the 5000 Lindy copies that she had created to help process paperwork. Sounds of typing echoed in the vast space. Lines of the recently dead waited for their papers to be processed.

There had been a few wars in the time Lindy had been running her little space of the infinitely expanding multiverse. Wars had the tendency to make the wait times longer, which were nearing 250 years as an influx of the newly dead poured in.

Lindy watched the bleak hellscape of streamlined bureaucracy. A slowly forming headache suddenly became a migraine. Lindy's eyes snapped to a distant corner of a familiar universe. The things that lurked between her multiverse and others had tried to make a foothold after a small incursion into the realm where Lindy had lived as a mortal. Each time they tried to break through again, Lindy had shut down their attempts, but this time was different: a single beast plugged a breach near a lonely world and began to infect the creatures there, making their souls toxic to Lindy and uninfected mortals. The infection swept that world; Lindy would be risking all she had built to counter the extra-dimensional beast directly, as it hid within the lone world that was now cut off from her influence. Brute-forcing her way through would only hurt Lindy and her universes.

Frost, Fate, and War arrived soon after the infection. They were people Lindy had known as mortals until their past world's World Spirits.

"What happened?" Fate demanded.

"Something broke through and cut me off." Lindy sighed as she leaned back in her chair.

Frost (whose proper title was Water, the element in her control) had a good idea what her closet companion was dealing with. Frost had spent many lives running after Lindy's trail of destruction back when they had a life. "You need to send mortals but don't want to risk this getting worse faster."

War crossed her arms. "You are getting soft, Uncle." War's attitude reminded Lindy of a connection they had in one of their previous lives when War felt Lindy was being stupid.

Lindy waved her arm dismissively across her mahogany desk at the lines of dead mortals glancing at them. "Do you have any idea the amount of paperwork this adds?"

"It affects all of us, so you will have help," Fate shot back.

War groaned, but Fate nudged her. War grabbed a bottle of Lindy's beer and chugged it, forgetting that the more one wanted to get tipsy in Death's realm, the more sober they would become, and the more they wanted good alcohol, the worse it would be. War gagged for a few seconds before looking at Lindy's shit-eating grin. "The last few economic stimulus plans went off the rails. I'll help too, but what's the real issue?"

Fate and Frost had to roll their eyes, for War's economic stimulus could mean anything from helping mortals invent things, to finding raw resources, to going to war. "She wants to avoid waking our child up," Frost sighed.

Long ago, Lindy's second attempt at creating a lesser copy of herself to help with tasks had used some of Frost's blood as well. The creation still floated in a vat hidden deep under the ruins of a cathedral that now was in the middle of a museum and troll sanctuary. "Is it so wrong to not want her to see how unkind the world is?" Lindy asked.

"For the last time, yes, it is. Wake her up, let her make mistakes and go to school, and let her live her own life. Plus if you are going to trust anyone with this, then trust her. It will be dangerous, but when she succeeds, the rules should let us give her something we can't otherwise." The topic of letting the copy that shared Frost's blood out of suspended animation was a topic that had strained Lindy and Frost's relationship over time. Lindy knew Frost was right but also wanted to shield that one copy from pain and sadness.

Lindy slowly nodded. "All right. You were always right, but this is the best solution. I have someone I can send her to. Give me a few days to set this up."

"I'll help," Frost replied. She knew how Lindy felt, but this was the best way of forcing the mortals to take care of the extra-dimensional creature living rent-free somewhere in their universe. War and Fate departed for their own realms.

Frost made a few cups of coffee. Somehow being a World Spirit of water allowed Frost to make the only good coffee available in Lindy's realm. As a middle manager from another department, Frost also did not have to wait a few hundred years for a coffee break, so she served coffee to Lindy's pen pushers and kept the lines in order as Lindy set up their plans.

Sometime later in Death's realm, a small form appeared near Lindy's desk. It looked like Lindy's second body except for the white hair and icy blue eyes, which were Frost's influence. "Do you understand me?" Lindy asked as she prodded the soul before her for damage.

While Lindy studied the soul before her, she was remotely controlling the partial copy's real body.

"Am I dead?" the soul asked.

Frost came over and raised an eyebrow. Lindy said, "No, you are alive. Your name is Lintwo. Your origin is complicated. I'm remotely piloting you to someone I can trust you with. We also need to talk."

"So you won't be with me?" Lintwo pressed, tilting her head.

Lindy sighed. This was hard for her, but putting it off had made it worse. Frost hugged Lintwo as the child stared at Lindy. Lindy tried to smile. "I will keep an eye on you, but any universe would break if a World Spirit manifested into it. I know you understand the rules binding me."

"They are very wordy," Lintwo agreed.

"They are, but study them, all right? I'm only piloting your body due to a loophole. Trust me, there are a lot of loopholes if you know where to look when you need them." Lindy grinned honestly.

"Don't give her ideas now," Frost requested.

"She's young and was made from us, and you expect her to stay out of trouble?" Lindy chuckled, now getting comfortable in her clutch of humor.

Frost picked Lintwo up and sat the form on her lap. "She does not need to know that."

Lindy nodded at Frost, who sat across from her while holding Lintwo tightly. "I need the mortals to investigate and eliminate a threat I can't touch. You have 4000 years before the World Spirits' shifts change. The sooner the better, as the most I can do is reinforce the reality around the affected area of space. Did that knowledge transfer over?"

Lintwo's eyes lost focus as she considered some recently imparted knowledge: "Coordinates, transmission vectors, and threat details; payment details for job completion; technical info for starship design, terrestrial reactor, and large-scale habitation construction methods; a few abilities for accurate threat detection to my own person; and a decaying damage shield. Um, I have a bunch of other stuff. Fire let me resist temperature and disease, War gave me the ability to always make and find money, Fate just made me extremely lucky, Earth made sure I'm always physically fit, and Air let me move really fast. Um, I also know all of the World Spirits' embarrassing secrets and can conjure water."

"Just don't use those secrets for blackmail material," Frost said. He was glad the others had given Lintwo some gifts.

"You gave her those secrets," Lindy sighed.

"I just thought, what would Lindy do?" Frost laughed.

Lindy rolled her eyes and placed a matte-black dagger that seemed to absorb light onto the desk. "This dagger is known as The End. We won't be able to talk much until the targets are dealt with, but this knife was made by your last words, Death, and has my power in it as well. It's very dangerous, so be careful. You will find it in your shadow." Lindy noticed Frost giving her the stink-eye. "Someday you will find it," Lindy added.

"Ok, any last advice?" Lintwo asked as she looked around Lindy's domain.

Frost gave Lintwo a tight hug. "Don't work yourself too hard."

"Enjoy everything you can and learn to accept the rest," Lindy said before waving her hand. "Ok, I got your real body where it needs to go. Don't give your brother too much trouble."

1

One Way Out

At the same time Lindy was talking to Lintwo deep in a hidden room in the afterlife, an ancient device broke as a slim hand cracked through a tank whose glass had fogged over long ago, in the physical realm.

Lindy emerged out of the tank in Lintwo's body. It was a remote connection using the barest trace of Death's power; metal around her rusted and the stone slowly turned to sand.

As she looked at the old and nostalgic lab, Lindy sidestepped without conscious thought. Half a second later, a ceiling panel that was more rust than steel impacted where Lintwo's body had been. "Crap, well, no time for sightseeing." Lindy sighed, then began to cough, as Lintwo's body had not spoken once, even though it was technically over 1000 years old.

Lindy pushed the body to run. It had been a long time since Lindy had inhabited a real flesh-and-blood form, plus Lintwo's body was stiff. Lindy's old instincts served her well, and the rain of debris was brief. After she rushed out into an old arena, the short-lived collapse stopped. The arena was covered in a thick layer of dust, but Lindy found the exit was still in the same place. However, the door was sealed.

Lindy looked back; through the billowing dust she had kicked up, many memories flashed through her mind. *Woodrow and Lintwo will need to live their own lives. I'll just give them as much support as I can and hope for the best.* Lindy mused as she rusted a very new lock to dust.

Lindy stepped out of the door and up some steps into a room filled with filing cabinets set between graves. The files contained data on the dead. Two slightly newer sarcophagi housed some of Lindy's past bodies.

Lindy walked up the steps. All the graves on each floor were exhaustively cataloged. The notes about her own past bodies were funny, as the currently accepted conjectures Lindy knew were around 80% bullshit. The few interviews with people who had known her over the ages were dismissed one way or another.

After many floors of catacombs, Lindy reached a newer vault door. The door was too well sealed to slip through using shadows. Lindy casually destroyed the lock and alarm systems, then left, destroying every camera she came across.

After leaving the old building, Lindy looked back at the ruins of a cathedral. It had been ransacked in a riot hundreds of years before and then left as it was, with repairs every few years to hold the crumbling building together. Officially it was kept this way as a testament to the folly of unthinking violence. In truth it was because those at the helm of the world's only two religions knew Lindy, and were at a loss of what to do when she became a World Spirit. Lindy had always been adamant that she was not any kind of all-powerful or all-knowing super entity worthy of worship. All Lindy ever wanted was to live, but as a Death, that desire was fulfilled in the most annoying way possible for her. After all, immortality was boring no matter how hard Lindy tried to laugh at it.

The hill the cathedral was on was no longer so lonely; at least a museum and wildlife sanctuary surrounded it.

Lindy walked towards the wildlife sanctuary. It was not technically the most direct route to Woodrow's home, but this sanctuary was the only place trolls still lived in the world, and it had been a long time since Lindy had seen one up close.

Lindy avoided the few cameras around, taking full advantage of Lintwo's small body. The guards were a joke. Even after a little over 1000 years, Lindy still could be silent if she wanted to be, plus the shadows responded even more fluidly than the last time she walked this world.

The steel and glass sanctuary was simple to break into. All it took was watching one guard punch a code into a keypad to bypass the external staff-only doors.

The inside was even simpler to sneak in, as the guards' footsteps made noise on the thick wooden visitor areas and tiled staff rooms.

When Lindy got to the visitor viewing areas, she found the one-way plastic windows placed high above the trolls' habitats to be agreeably sturdy.

The trolls slept, but a few began to have fitful dreams as the creatures felt the presence of a natural predator watching them calmly. None of these trolls had experienced being prey as their ancestors had.

Lindy felt a strong concentration of shadow and death energies rushing toward her. It was likely one of the few watchers Lindy had let roam this planet, so Lindy fled, wondering if this watcher would catch her in a far less powerful body.

Lindy stopped when she found an exhibit. Old bits of armor, a mockup of a dwarven furnace, and a whole section on mines stood out, but in the far corner was a long black coat Lindy had not seen in a long time, one that Lintwo could fit in. The coat fell into its own shadow and appeared around Lintwo's body. The steps of one of her watchers rushing over drew nearer, so Lindy fled again. She was slowly getting used to what Lintwo's body could do.

Lindy slipped out of the building and moved swiftly down the hill into a sprawling city of steel, glass, and concrete. A few stone buildings Lindy recognized still stood, but most of the old buildings had been damaged in one war or another, and a few had been modified or torn down once people no longer cared about their history or that history became inconvenient. The world's first train station had been torn down because its use in war was inconvenient, but many new train stations had replaced it, while a few of the first factories that mass-produced guns were still in use with their insides updated.

The night welcomed Lintwo and Lindy, letting them slip through the still congested city. Cars and trucks sped by on well-maintained roads while drunks stumbled along sidewalks and crosswalks.

Lindy observed that her city seemed far more alive than it had been when she was still mortal. Humans, elves, dragons in bipedal form, orcs, goblins, ogres, dwarves, beast folk, and shades all walked by her as Lindy zeroed in on a familiar aura.

At an old but well-maintained apartment building, Lindy slipped through the locked front door when a human woman opened it. The human did not notice Lindy as they walked up a few flights of stairs and to the same door.

Lindy knocked on the door, causing the human to notice her for the first time. The door swiftly opened. Lindy's son Woodrow stood in the doorway. He was lightly dressed. "Stacy, welcome back." Woodrow smiled. Lindy smelled a stew and other food wafting from her son's apartment.

Stacy looked down at Lindy, causing Woodrow to lock eyes with Lintwo's body. Woodrow could feel his parent's judgment. "Woodrow, we need to talk," Lindy said, still not used to Lintwo's voice sounding far more like Frost's.

"Do I know you?" Woodrow asked.

Lindy grinned in the mad way only she really seemed to do. "I think you do. Your sister is alive now, and I need a favor."

Woodrow dragged both his girlfriend Stacy and Lindy into the apartment, then shut the door. "Your name now."

"This body belongs to your sister Lintwo, but I wanted to check on you, Woodrow. Your last wife died 512 years ago. I'm not judging you. How much does Stacy know about the family? How much does she know about Lindy?"

Stacy looked between her boyfriend and the odd person that looked slightly like him. "The Death god?"

"I'm not a god." Lindy sighed at the same time as Woodrow agreed, "She's very different from what the cult of Shrew says."

Stacy looked down at Lindy, who explained, "He is right about that. Anyway, I don't have much time before I need to get back to my realm and put my daughter back in this body."

"Wait, I need a beer first," Woodrow said, turning around. "Sit anywhere, Pops," he said, walking away.

Lindy looked around. "It's a long story," she said as she sat on a very nice leather recliner.

Stacy took one more look at Lindy before going to grab something stronger than a beer.

Woodrow and Stacy sat across from Lindy. "Short version, Woodrow. I need you to take care of your half-sister for a few years. I'll get your expenses reimbursed."

"My sister is the one that's been under the cathedral for the past, what, 1000 years?" Woodrow asked.

"It's been a little over that," Lindy explained.

"Wait, you are Death, and he's over 1000?" Stacy asked.

"That's right." Lindy nodded before looking at Woodrow.

"I'll answer all your questions after this," Woodrow promised Stacy.

"Good, you clearly trust her enough to have been living together for the past three years." Lindy smiled but raised her hands when the two younger people glared at her. "A parent worries, all right?"

"Fine, so how long do I need to help?" Woodrow asked.

"Until Lintwo can stand on her own. She will need a crash course in current academics up to middle school level and a few years of high school after that. I'm hoping she should be able to manage college on her own," Lindy replied.

"Fine, I'll help, but only because she's family." Woodrow nodded.

"Good. Then I'm leaving and putting Lintwo back in this body." Lindy smiled before closing her eyes.

2

The Start of New Things

Lintwo opened her eyes, now in her own body. Woodrow and Stacy both looked over from the kitchen table, having finished dinner and a long talk about the past. "Ok, um, nice to meet you, brother?" Lintwo asked tentatively.

Woodrow got up and walked over to Lintwo; he knew it would take time getting used to being a brother. "How are you feeling?" he asked.

Lintwo thought for a few seconds. "Like I woke up after sleeping for a very long time, I think? Feeling things is still very new to me, but I understand the concept."

Stacy called over from the table, "You and I are going clothes shopping tomorrow, just the two of us."

"Thank you?" Lintwo said.

Stacy got up and walked to the kitchen doorway. "You can call me Stacy. If you can, get some rest." With that, Stacy walked to the apartment's only bedroom.

"It's been a crazy day for all of us. The couch folds out, and there is some stew in the fridge. Do you need anything else tonight?" Woodrow smiled. His night had been a little stressful, but he mostly blamed Lindy for that.

"I should be fine for the night, thank you," Lintwo said as she looked around the room.

"I'll show you how the appliances work tomorrow. Good night." Woodrow smiled before going to bed.

The next morning breakfast was quiet. Woodrow gave his sister some clothes his children had once worn.

A few of Woodrow's younger kids were still alive, and he had many grandchildren, but as he got older, Woodrow had come to respect Lindy more and understand why she felt so alone. Woodrow was the closest to immortal anyone in the world ever had been, other than Lindy. After all, Woodrow did have it on good authority that while he did not age, he could die.

Woodrow left for his job as a security guard at a car park across from the college he had once run.

Stacy called in sick to her job. She hoped to avoid seeing any of her coworkers, and with how bewildered Lintwo was about even a microwave, Stacy was hoping her new shopping buddy could rein in some of the awe, as it was very eye-catching. Stacy double-checked her travel supplies and the expiration date on her pepper spray.

Stacy led Lintwo out of the apartment. They walked to the subway with the rest of the early commuters. Normally the ogres stood out the most, given how huge they were, but somehow Lintwo in her old hand-me-down dress stood out the most. There was just something otherworldly about her.

Lintwo stayed close as they bought a ticket. The old shade at the counter kept her eyes on Lintwo the entire time.

The day got stranger as they waited for the train. The people on the platform parted. Even Stacy felt the need to move aside as something approached, but Lintwo stood her ground and held Stacy's hand, stopping her from fleeing.

One of Death's watchers walked up to Lintwo and glanced at Stacy. "Your aura is hurting them. Stop it!" Lintwo demanded as she glared at the watcher.

Up close Lintwo almost looked like a younger version of the watcher. "Very well." The watcher choked on the rest of its sentence.

This was a very odd scene, as no one sane spoke down to a watcher, and very few ever tried to order them around. Watchers were rare and respected. Every watcher looked like a past version of Lindy, the human that became Death itself, and each watcher had similar but heavily weakened versions of a few of the powers Lindy had when she walked the world.

The scars Lindy had left on the land, foremost among them the wasteland and the Maw, a pit that ate magic, were more than enough for anything closely related to her to be met with fear, respect, and sometimes reverence.

The watcher winced as her creator made it very clear to not cause trouble for Lintwo or Woodrow.

"Right, so, um, where are you going?" the watcher asked.

"Shopping for clothes," Stacy squeaked out as the watcher tilted its head to regard her.

The lights in the station flickered. "No bad, Stacy is safe," Lintwo growled.

The watcher seemed to deflate. "Very well, but I am coming with you."

Lintwo held out her hand. "Good, then teach me how to blend in better."

The watcher awkwardly shook Lintwo's hand. "Let's take a taxi, then I'll cover the cost."

The watcher kept hold of Lintwo, who kept hold of Stacy as they left the station. A few blocks later, they had lost the handful of stupidly brave people who tried to follow them. As they walked, the watcher showed Lintwo how to dampen their natural presence enough to still be seen but not recognized for what they were.

After the watcher had dampened her presence enough, she took off her coat and put on glasses. Stacy had to double-take. A person who could be anywhere from 18 to 34 with long black hair wearing a gray pinstripe business suit stood before her. The watcher now looked exactly like Stacy's direct boss.

"We saw each other just yesterday, Stacy. I see you have an ironclad reason for calling in sick," the watcher said calmly as they arrived at a taxi stand.

"Wait, you are the real Lexi?" Stacy asked.

"That's right. It looks like I'm taking a sick day too. Rock is going to put that management seminar to work sooner than planned," Lexi the watcher said as she texted work quickly.

"I'm Lintwo, by the way," the oldest out of the three of them announced.

"I know, Elder, I know," Stacy said, expecting Lindy to shout in her mind again but not getting anything too obvious.

A taxi quickly arrived. The commuter traffic began to thin around the time they reached the mall.

Lexi paid close attention to the small number of shoppers and staff in the mall. She felt out of her depth. Her instinct told her to protect Lintwo at all costs from anything that looked harmful. There were few issues with this; Lexi was not a bodyguard in any way. All she had done for 1000 years was keep an eye on the natives of this world, blend in, and kill a few that tried to cheat Death after their time should have been up. The main issue was a little simpler: the current Death did not want the watchers giving Lintwo special treatment.

Lintwo, Lexi, and Stacy walked through a barrier of some kind and found themselves in an empty version of the mall. All three were immediately on guard and stood their ground. Lintwo and Lexi kept Stacy between them.

Two mannequins shambled out of a shop. One mannequin held a scale, the other a blank coffee mug that kept changing color. "Took you long enough," the scale-holding one seemed to say despite not having a mouth.

Dark smoke filled the odd space, and a chill breeze descended. "Oh, come on, that response was way too fast," the other mannequin replied.

Stacy felt herself pushed through a barrier. Her phone dinged with a text from an unknown number. *Wait there, I'll deal with this,* it said.

Back in the pocket dimension that looked like a mall, Lindy and Frost manifested. "Chaos, Order – it's been a while," Lindy said sternly.

"You are skirting the rules again. We had to check on the one you bent those rules for. You two can call me Chaos; everyone else does," the coffee-mug-holding mannequin noted.

"The less trendy one's Order," Lindy said, pointing at the scale-holding mannequin.

"So why the special treatment?" Order demanded.

"One of the outsider entities is trying to manifest in this universe. We needed someone we can trust but not directly connected to us to deal with it," Frost said.

"And you could not empower some random person with a ton of power and send them at the issue?" Chaos asked.

Lindy shrugged. "That tends to not end the way the giver of that power intends."

"Right, I should not be asking the poster child of powered-up randoms." Chaos shrugged.

"Just be careful. We can't allow too many more exceptions." Order facepalmed.

Lintwo and Lexi were shoved back out of the pocket dimension and found themselves next to Stacy.

Lintwo stared into space. "I need something sweet or a cold juice after that."

"Agreed. We passed an ice cream parlor..." Lexi replied.

Lintwo and Lexi downed two root beer floats each, while Stacy nursed an apple juice, trying to come to terms with how crazy her life had suddenly become.

"So the elves at Woodrow's family gatherings?" Stacy whispered but paused midway.

Lexi finished her sentence. "Are his descendants?"

"If it means anything, no matter what my folks say, you two seem good together," Lintwo noted.

"But why are you here, boss?" Stacy asked.

"I'm assigned to this city, and while the watchers have standing orders not to interfere with our original children, we only found out her daughter is active after I met you two." Lexi sighed.

"That's a lot to take in," Stacy replied, shaking her head.

"Look on the bright side: while my folks need to be impartial, it can't hurt to be on Death's good side," Lintwo said, trying to cheer up her brother's girlfriend.

Stacy gave Lintwo a long searching look. "Right, no pressure," she deadpanned.

"Oh very good, I like you too," Lintwo giggled, looking like the spitting image of Lindy.

Lexi shook her head. "All right, Stacy. I'll see you tomorrow." Lexi paid for her meal and beat a hasty retreat. Lintwo had begun to trigger a few flashbacks to the few times Lexi had seen her boss show strong emotion, which always made a lasting impact.

Stacy chose not to question anything else that day. After paying for the meal and some clothes for Lintwo, they took another taxi back home.

It was decided that Lintwo would be homeschooled for a year to bring her up to speed on current events, advancements, and the history of the last four millennia.

Lintwo had an understanding of the world until right before the creation of the wasteland. Other than that, she had a few observations from multiple people and viewpoints from only the last 1000 years. Most of those observations and viewpoints were contradictory on some level.

Lintwo was given books, assignments, and a crash course in computers along with access to a laptop. Lexi stopped by every so often to help review info. Stacy helped teach Lintwo about modern technology and culture. Only Woodrow and the watchers could really understand and empathize with how lost Lintwo felt about the modern world, which was sometimes what Lintwo really needed.

Something Lexi let slip once stuck with Lintwo. As far as Lexi understood them, the World Spirit rules were fairly basic, not counting a list of caveats and examples that were just asking to be exploited. The rule was a World Spirit maintained the influence of their concept and processed tasks in the background to maintain a smooth-running existence of the multiverse, while not directly interfering with the mortal world. Any anomalies in the mortal world that needed to be corrected required surrogates or other outside contracted help, but for the most part the World Spirits' actual influence was expected to passively affect the universes they were assigned to. The only real perk besides being more or less immortal and having the ability to take a break every few hundred years was that every 5000 years, the World Spirits that had served at least 5000 years had a wrap-up party where they would be reassigned to five new realities.

Time moved onward, and soon Lintwo's first day of high school began. The watchers had worked in the background to make a paper trail for Lintwo that would allow her to appear to have lived as a human for 14 years.

Lintwo's grades from homeschooling were very good, which gave the watchers extra work, as they had to bump the averages of her (fictitious) middle school level grades up without causing any troublesome questions or making their influence known.

Near the edge of Lindy's old city's borders, and a stone's throw from the wasteland, sat a high school built on land that had once been a train depot during a war and sold for cheap when public opinion on that war took a nose dive. The school was creatively named Good Crossing High. A few factories surrounded the school, and one of the city's bus lines, called the brown line, had its second-to-last stop in a roundabout near the school.

Before the sun had risen, Lintwo stood at the bus stop. Stacy had begun to think of Lintwo as her daughter and hugged Lintwo as the bus approached. Lintwo patted Stacy on the back, wishing her brother would just propose already.

The bus was packed with a few office staff, some factory workers, and a bunch of high school students with backpacks who mostly clustered in the back of the bus. The small gaggle of office staff took the middle of the bus near the back doors, while the factory workers took up the entire front. There were no rules stating who sat where, but it had just become tradition over the years. Lintwo sat on the imaginary line between the high schoolers and office workers.

Over the next few stops the office workers trickled out, and more students entered, filling up those spots. A dragon in human form sat next to Lintwo. The dragon looked like a 10-year-old human girl with horns, a few scales, and a tail.

Dragons and elves physically aged more slowly than humans, but the tradeoff was they lived far longer. Dragons were well known for their brute strength and toughness, even in human form.

"You smell odd," the dragon girl told Lintwo.

"And you smell like fire and brimstone," Lintwo replied, holding out her hand. "I'm Lintwo. What are you called?" The two shook hands, neither using too much strength in case they wound up hurting the other.

"You can call me Qilpeea Sagezard. Are you a mage?" the dragon asked. She was sure she had cleaned off, but Qilpeea's elders told her once that her magic smelled like lava. Qilpeea believed her magic smelled like tulips and that Lintwo smelled like decay and rust, but knew that could be her fellow student's magic.

Mages were rare, but there were a few others that smelled off to Qilpeea. Hopefully that was just their magic, but none of the student mages had learned to sense magic and the world at the same time. An old adage went something like "A mage is a mage because they sense magic at all times."

Of all the students, Qilpeea and Lintwo had the most skill with magic. Qilpeea sat next to Lintwo for two reasons: one, she was a stranger (most of the students had gone to one of three middle schools); and two, Lintwo smelled dangerous. The other student mages kept their non-mage classmates away from Lintwo. Magic that caused death and decay was disliked, feared, and respected in Qilpeea's clan. A few of her ancestors had even fought with Death's herald long ago.

At the school bus stop, all the students and most of the factory staff got off. Lintwo noticed the other students were trying to avoid her, so Lintwo stayed close to Qilpeea.

Teachers herded the students into the auditorium. Qilpeea took Lintwo's hand and sat her at one end of the front row, then sat next to her. "The magic-sensitive students, including myself, are scared of how your magic feels. They should warm up to you in time."

A few of the older elf and dragon teachers kept an eye on Lintwo. The headmaster was a very old shade; it took all his will not to stare at Lintwo. For some of the more knowledgeable teachers, it was not just how Lintwo's magic felt but also how she looked. As for those that knew about Lindy and the watchers, Lintwo had far more than a passing resemblance to them, plus very few parents would use Lin as part of a child's name.

The headmaster's speech was mostly a review of class schedules and how to contact the school. He finished with an announcement that the first field trip of the year would be in three weeks.

All the magic-sensitive students were put in the same class. All the other young mages knew each other, as even if they went to different schools, the state mandated that magic users undergo tests. Magic was far rarer and weaker than it had been, but also more volatile, meaning anyone able to use magic needed to learn early on how to use it safely, which created an industry of private coaches, gyms, dojos, and medical officers that specialized in teaching them.

Most elves and dragons could use some magic, but for everyone else, magic ability was random and not hereditary at all. Oddly, elves and dragons were still the longest-lived, but now they became ill more often, so most elves and dragons did not die of old age but of sickness.

Over the next few days Lintwo got used to class and mostly kept to herself while trying to be kind, patient, and nonthreatening.

Lintwo learned a few things. The most notable was that the agents of the world spirits were no longer called priestesses but were now called advocates and that Death was the only one that called them watchers.

Lintwo had four classes a day, rotating between gym, math, science, literature, history, and magic theory. The classes rotated seemingly at random; the only constant was magic theory, which took most of the school day and consisted of lessons on the kinds of magic, their use in the modern world, and tips on how to cast safely.

Notable mages were used as examples. Lindy was the only ancient example of a notable shadow magic user, but a few shades were used as contemporary examples.

The day before the first field trip, Lintwo was listening to another example of her parent: "Lindy created the pit in the center of our city. After that, magic weakened gradually." Most of the students were looking at Lintwo and not the teacher, which had happened whenever her creator was name-dropped. Lindy had come up many times in history class as well, with the same reactions. "Some accounts say that at the time Lindy fought an army; others say she was in a rush. We may never know the full story."

An Earth mage named Jim Dandy raised their hand. "Why don't we ask then?"

Samandrea Thillmore, the only advocate of a World Spirit in class, was chosen by Fate and noted, "The World Spirits don't answer just any question."

"But we have a watcher in class, right?" Jim pressed petulantly.

Lintwo sighed. These conversations had become more common as the days rolled on. She had tried to ignore them, but her annoyance had reached a breaking point. "That's news to me," Lintwo growled.

A few students were about to argue, but Jim smiled smugly. "Then you are just a pretender."

The room was suddenly covered in a rippling shadow that ripped like tar. "This is the last time I will remind you, I am not a watcher." Lintwo whispered these words, but the wall reverberated and amplified them.

The teacher was the first to get his fear under control. "Deep breaths. Control your power."

Qilpeea touched Lintwo's shoulder gently. Lintwo could feel her friend's terror as Qilpeea tried to not shake too much. Lintwo took a few deep breaths, and the shadows receded.

"Jim, Lintwo, that was dangerous. I'm going to have to talk to your parents this weekend," the teacher said, almost managing to sound stern.

A few seconds later, Samandrea jolted as though struck by lightning. Samandrea rubbed her head and proclaimed quietly, "That's not a good idea." Without bothering to explain further, Samandrea got out of her seat. "I don't feel well." She left the class and went to the nurse.

Samandrea had heard Fate's voice a handful of times; every other time Fate had sounded all-knowing, unflappable, and completely in control. The panicked urgency of the message Fate had just sent troubled Samandrea. It was not even prophetic but sounded like someone did a spit take and groaned, "They are not going to like that. Damn it, I hope she does not show up. That bumbling fool! It looks like game day is going to be an intervention again." Fate had kept ranting in Samandrea's head all day to the point where she had to go home early. Other voices crept into Fate's progressively unhinged rant until the one Fate had spent the last hour yelling at drunkenly laughed, "You think I'm unprofessional? You left that one on all day, old friend." After an audible click, Samandrea could no longer hear the World Spirits' importunate party, but she still stayed up all night wondering what the hell she had just listened to and coming to terms with Fate being more human than Samandrea liked to believe.

Around the same time, Lintwo was eating dinner with her brother and Stacy. The doorbell rang. Woodrow answered it cautiously while Lintwo trailed behind him curiously. Two mannequins sat in front. Outside, Lexi stood next to them, looking far more haggard than when Stacy had seen her a few hours before. "These may walk out sometime tomorrow. Don't ask."

"More World Spirit shenanigans?" Woodrow asked as he poked the mannequins.

Stacy and Lexi winced. It was common belief that any disrespect to a World Spirit, especially directly disrespecting them by name or title, was a very bad idea. More than a few house fires were blamed on people indirectly insulting the World Spirit of Fire, to the extent that any insinuation that a heater, stove, or furnace could spontaneously erupt into flames was frowned upon, as it was believed that Fire might take that as an invitation to make that insinuation come true.

Lexi shook her head free of thoughts and left. Woodrow and Lintwo moved the mannequins inside.

The next day on the bus to school, Qilpeea sat next to Samandrea, who had not slept at all the night before. Lintwo sat by herself pretending not to see the two figures who'd covered their whole bodies with heavy clothes sitting near the front of the bus.

When they arrived at the school stop, Lintwo grabbed Qilpeea and Samandrea and dragged them swiftly to the side. One of the suspicious heavily clothed figures turned to them. Samandrea and Qilpeea flinched seeing the figure's eyes and knowing they and the area around them were artificial. Lintwo tapped her neck where the figure's sky mask exposed one of the mannequin's joints. When the figure fixed the mask, Lintwo whispered, "You need dark sunglasses or something too." Reflective sunglasses materialized over the mannequin's eyes. "Good enough. Just don't mess up too bad, please? I am starting to like it here." The mannequin patted Lintwo, Qilpeea, and Samandrea on their heads before being dragged off by the other one.

Qilpeea shook. "What was that?" she hissed.

"My parents seem to have taken yesterday as a challenge or an excuse for a short vacation," Lintwo replied as she held her friends up to prevent them from falling to their knees.

"We are so dead. Do you know what that was?" Samandrea asked.

Lintwo liked Qilpeea and Samandrea. "Promise me to keep a secret?"

"Do I have a choice?" Samandrea asked.

"Yes?" Lintwo asked, unsure if that was true. She felt that it would be a bad idea to use her parents' influence, but at the same time the World Spirits were watching her. Their interest had always been a double-edged sword if history and the knowledge Lintwo had been given were anything to go by. Lintwo hoped none of the World Spirits had bragged about her to any of their advocates yet. Fate luckily seemed level-headed, so Lintwo felt it was unlikely Samandrea knew very much.

Qilpeea pulled away from Lintwo and managed to stand on two feet. "Just tell us why we are hiding."

Lintwo took a deep breath, hoping her friends would take her biggest secret well. "The World Spirits of Death and Water are technically my biological parents."

Qilpeea looked at Lintwo like she was crazy. "Um, sure?" the dragon said.

Samandrea pushed Lintwo. "That explains a lot, but I really don't want to know any more."

Samandrea began to stumble over to the school's front door. "Um, waiting outside may be a good idea," Lintwo said.

"Why?" Samandrea snapped.

"My folks' temporal forms are still inside?" Lintwo replied. Samandrea scampered back over and hid behind Qilpeea.

Soon after the teachers and other students came out of the building, a few teachers avoided looking at Lintwo. None of the staff spoke to Lintwo, Qilpeea, or Samandrea about waiting outside. Many other students took note of this, and Lintwo knew it would be used against her later in one way or another.

The other students avoided Lintwo and company as much as they could. "Looks like we are sitting together," Qilpeea observed as they waited in line to get on the buses.

Samandrea groaned but was too tired to do much else. Mercifully she was able to sit between Qilpeea and Lintwo as they were driven to a nature reserve for the forest trip.

3

Old Sins

The bus drove along a route through the wasteland, which was still a blasted, sand-covered hellscape with next to no life even after thousands of years. The city had two suburbs in the wasteland. Some towns also sat near the old rail lines, but other than that, only a handful of small critters placed there by beings with opposable thumbs lived there.

The nature reserve sat on the edge of the wasteland near an industrial park. Thick green trees and other foliage clashed with warehouses and the desolate landscape next to it all. A tall mesh fence with a three-foot stone base surrounded the reserve.

As they neared the reserve, Lintwo was sure she was being watched from behind the fence.

At the gates stood three park rangers. One had his arm in a sling. A sign on the ticket counter helpfully informed visitors that the last workplace injury was three days before and the last death was 50 years ago.

The students hopped out of their buses and were split into two groups by class. The magic-using students were placed with two other classes with the highest grades and led by a younger ranger. The other five classes were assigned to the most experienced ranger on site, while the injured one manned the ticket booth.

The forest was thick and unseasonably green. Lintwo felt intense gazes from two directions deeper in the woods directed at her.

Their guide stopped at a sign that stood at a fork in the path. The forest's feel and look were split from that point on. On one side the trees were flowering with dense green vines and unmarred bark; the other side was covered in slightly twisted dark thorns. The trees had bite marks, some of which looked to have been caused by large fanged jaws, and thin dark vines grew from larger bites, coiling around the trees.

The guide pointed to the more chaotic path. "The twist sprite habitat is that way." And then to the more verdant one. "The dryad enclave is down that path. From here on, be careful not to stray from the marked paths."

A dark imp-like thing that was almost all maw, fang, and barbs landed on Lintwo's head. "This one visits us first, yes, yes?" A few more twist sprites appeared, each with their own slightly disquieting appearance, the only commonality being the ability to expand their jaws to at least five times their body size.

The guide looked at Lintwo, who was more amused than anything else but tried to look annoyed as her inherited memories told her to. Lintwo patted a few of the other twist sprites around her. "Are you ok?" the guide asked, feeling a little weirded out at how docile the magic and insane little gremlins were being for once.

A light airy cough was heard, and a dryad, which looked like a tree in the shape of a human wearing a thin cloak of leaves, stood on the dryad path. "When you visit, don't bring the twisted ones." With that, the dryad walked into one of the trees, seemingly being absorbed by it.

Dryads had only been legally considered people for 500 years after a large fire caused by reckless campers exterminated three large dryad tribes. A dryad leader led protests, and when that did not work, the dryads caused bad harvests by controlling plant life. Dryads were granted citizenship by the World Council in all its member states. Dryads physically could not live in cities; they needed to be in places with lots of vegetation.

Incidentally, the World Council was composed of the leaders of each nation, and they are still to this day more terrified of the World Spirits than anyone else.

To the guides' credit, they only gave the twist sprites a sideways glance before leading the group into the darker half of the forest.

The foliage became even more gnarled the deeper they went.

A swarm of twist sprites soon formed around Lintwo. Twist sprites were always a menace. They loved pranks, had a huge appetite, and twisted plant life into cruel-looking forms. Mages were also sometimes accidentally affected by such changes, but in cases where an individual legally considered a person was affected (and sometimes when an intelligent being not legally considered a person, such as a treant, was affected), a watcher would always arrive to see how the change happened, try to heal the individual if asked to, and interrogate the sprites responsible.

The fact that the sprites restrained their chaos and followed Lintwo's orders was a level of respect not even watchers were given, even though Death created them both (along with the original shades), which was very suspicious.

The guide pointed out the changed foliage, explaining what the plants once were and what they had become. Western oak trees had twelve different known variants after being exposed to twist sprites. Most of the changed plants were poisonous, but the park rangers removed the dangerous ones to the surrounding area.

Samandrea reached out to touch one of the sprites flittering around Lintwo. The sprite growled. "That one is ok, so play nice," Lintwo admonished.

The sprite allowed itself to be petted by Samandrea while the others moved to hover higher above the visitors.

Jim tried to touch the sprite that was begrudgingly allowing Samandrea to pet it. Lintwo caught Jim's hand. "Don't make these critters more agitated."

"But they follow your orders," Jim snapped.

"They are not my slaves or underlings," Lintwo explained as she let go of Jim's hand.

"Then why do they listen to you?" Jim asked as he rubbed his hand.

The sprites collectively leered at Jim. "Fear and home," they tittered before deciding they had enough of Lintwo's fellows. The twist sprites flew off into the dingy woods.

The guide soon stopped at a white line cut into the dirt path. "We turn around here."

As the group began to turn, a feeling overcame Lintwo, causing her to move before thinking about it. She tapped her chest, drawing a survival knife from the sheath that seemed to absorb all light. Lintwo sunk into a shadow from her place near the middle of the clump of students only to leap out near the edge of the group. Her blade flashed, striking down a spine of healthy-looking wood.

Instinctively Lintwo searched for the source of the attack. Lintwo had inherited some of the combat instincts and habits of the two that had been used to create her.

Samandrea and Qilpeea had only taken a few steps towards Lintwo when more spines flew at the class, in a wider arc this time. Lintwo growled as her conscious mind was slowly suppressed, replaced by the instincts she had not been prepared or trained to control.

Twist sprites erupted from the woods. The words "kill," "eat," and "hunt" made up most of the sprites' disjointed chorus.

Lintwo's conscious mind wrestled for some control before her overpowering combat instincts took over. She pointed at her group. "Protect," Lintwo managed to choke out before her legs decided to take her into the woods, beelining to the source of the attack.

Lintwo rushed past twisted vines and thorn-covered trees. More spines flew at her from the dryad side of the park. Between the foliage and her knife, no spines interrupted Lintwo's momentum.

Knife in hand, Lintwo burst into a clearing just on the dryad side. The other school group lay unconscious in the open with no visible guards.

"Don't make me corrupt these trees just to find you," Lintwo called out into the healthier woodland. The wind shifted slightly, and a cloud of sweet-smelling pollen washed over her. The pollen tasted like poison on her tongue.

Lintwo narrowed her eyes and forced ice to block off the clearing from the tree line. A wall of clear ice grew to just above the treetops. "Last chance to talk this out. We can always do this the hard way."

A dryad walked out of a tree and stood in front of the ice wall. "And why would we listen to his spawn?"

"What?" Lintwo asked before it clicked. "Oh, I'm Woodrow's half-sister, not his daughter."

"Impossible. There have not been any more twisted members of our kin," the dryad snapped haughtily.

Lintwo rolled her eyes. "Good for you, but I did not mean that half."

More dryads walked from the trees. "Then why do you smell like decay?" another one asked.

Lintwo groaned as her adrenaline high receded, replaced by annoyance. "Where do you think the Lin in Lintwo comes from?"

"Death herself," a dryad said swiftly.

"Right, so don't waste my time, and don't attack me or my brother's kid for some ancient grudge that none of them had a part in. You are mad at Death, so take it up with her," Lintwo explained. The dryads began to shift nervously, so Lintwo pressed on. "Let my classmates go. They have no part in this, and I will leave with them."

"You will stay," a few dryads replied.

Lintwo dropped the knife that had once belonged to Lindy into the dirt, causing the grass to twist and grow spines. After a small path was twisted, she kicked the blade back into her hand. "Do you want to see how fast I can change the rest of this place? Let us go."

The dryads fled, and soon after, their hostages woke up. "What happened?" the older ranger asked.

"Expect a watcher to come by and ask the staff here exactly that." Lintwo replied, and she turned to the still groggy teachers. "We should go." After the teachers agreed, the ice walls came down, and Lintwo walked back to the bus.

The ticket booth was empty, and the sign about injuries was changed from 3 to 0. A watcher Lintwo did not recognize waited by the park entrance. Lintwo tried not to think too hard about why the sign listing when the last death occurred was taken down.

When Lintwo got home, Stacy and Lexi were sitting at the kitchen table. Lexi was looking at the ceiling, and Stacy was looking into a half-full glass of water. Woodrow was nowhere to be seen. "We need to talk," Lexi said just as Lintwo entered.

Lintwo walked a few steps before both her caretakers looked over at her. "You mean me?" Lintwo sat down at the table; Stacy looked away.

"I have it on good authority some dryads tried to kill you," Lexi said.

"Is that why my brother is not here?" Lintwo asked.

"He chose to be left out of this. Your mother does not want to interfere or have you used to relying on her authority. The watchers know she cares, but Death has always been awkward about these things. If you ever need to talk to her while on this world, she will make time," Lexi grumbled.

"I know Lexi, thanks." Lintwo nodded.

Stacy shook her head. "Someone tried to kill you. How are you so calm?"

"I suppose I haven't thought about it yet? I didn't have time to think too much at the time. I had people to protect. The ones that got caught up in an attempt on my life came first," Lintwo said slowly as her eyes began to water, realizing that fact—her life had been targeted.

Lexi patted Lintwo on the back. "It's not your fault. No one should be held accountable for their ancestor's deeds."

"Maybe in a perfect world," Lintwo replied as she held back some until-then repressed emotions.

Stacy choked back her own choice words and said in a shaken tone that was meant to be even, "Dinner is in the fridge with your name on it. Tomorrow is the weekend. Sleep as long as you want."

"And if you ever need to talk, your family and I will be around," Lexi said.

Lintwo woke up mid-afternoon and found her lunch in the fridge. Her brother and Stacy sat on the couch watching the news. Lintwo sat with them in silence. Seemingly in no time, dinner came and went. Lintwo helped Woodrow wash the dishes. "Are you all right?" Woodrow asked, his voice sounding louder than it was after a day of relative silence.

"I'll be alright. I have some knowledge from both my folks, but I don't understand any of it. My body moved on its own, bro; that's the only reason I was not hurt," Lintwo said sadly.

"Did you enjoy fighting?" Woodrow asked.

Lintwo shook her head. "Fuck no, it was terrifying!"

"Language!" Stacy called from the kitchen table.

"You have not gotten used to combat, but taking lives is not something to enjoy. It will take a while, but find a balance," Woodrow advised.

"Sure," Lintwo nodded.

The next day Woodrow went to the park at the local government's request to talk to the dryads.

School on Monday was canceled, but a letter came for Woodrow inviting him to a family get-together.

"My descendants and some people who knew Lindy in life and their descendants get together every 10 years or so. I'd like for both of you to come with me," Woodrow announced at dinner.

"Sure, I'd like that," Lintwo agreed as she watched Stacy.

"Ok, is there anything I should know ahead of time?" Stacy asked.

"It's being held at an old manor in the wasteland. Most of the guests treat it as a semi-formal event, but clean casual clothes are fine." Woodrow shrugged.

"Just be yourself. Our parents never cared about appearances. If anyone gives you trouble, remind them of that," Lintwo added.

That night they found out that school had been canceled for the week and that counseling paid by the city was being offered. Lintwo stayed home for the most part, but one day at a mall she helped Stacy find something formal to wear plus a warm coat.

That weekend Woodrow drove them into the wasteland in his sport utility vehicle. The border of the wasteland was stark, going from green and steel to sand and rust. Even then, the cheapest neighborhoods sprawled over from the city.

There was no road to speak of deep in the wasteland; the dust storms had covered all of those completely. Woodrow drove along some old train tracks. Lintwo noted that even the air tasted stale, which brought into focus that the wasteland was truly a dead land. No plants grew, and everything rotted far faster than it should. Even animals aged faster within its borders. The magic-eating pit within Lintwo's home city seemed to have halted the wasteland's advance, at least.

As the family crested yet another sand dune, they spied a manor home with a fully manicured green yard, which stood out starkly in the sea of sand. A clean and tall wrought iron fence surrounded the manor. Other vehicles were parked just inside the fence near a hedge maze.

The gate opened on its own, allowing Woodrow to park near the other vehicles. "No questions yet?" Lintwo asked Stacy.

"Let me enjoy this party first," Stacy sighed. She expected something odd, but this manor was well outside her expectations.

"I trust both of you," Woodrow said before getting out.

"If it helps, I think our parent likes you two." Lintwo shrugged.

Stacy and Lintwo stood next to the car as Woodrow walked over to a small crowd standing near the hedge maze.

In the sky a flock of red dragons descended. The smallest of them was helped along by a slightly larger one.

The dragons transmuted into their humanoid forms right above the manor and landed near the vehicles with a small shockwave. Lintwo and Stacy held down their skirts as the wave passed.

"There they go again," an old elf near Woodrow called out.

"Damn right," a visibly aged dragon laughed. Both the elf and dragon were the oldest of their kind Lintwo had seen.

"Lintwo?" a familiar voice asked from the sill, dissipating the cloud of dust the dragons had created.

Lintwo turned to see Qilpeea staring at her. "Oh, you came with your family too?"

"Darling, is this the new friend you keep bragging about?" something that looked like an older version of Qilpeea asked.

"Moma!" Qilpeea called out in an agitated tone.

Lintwo tilted her head over at Woodrow. "I'm here with my brother. It's nice to meet you."

"Violet," Qilpee's mother said.

"I almost thought you guys gave up on the flowery names," Lintwo noted.

Woodrow walked over with a few shades and elves. Lintwo felt a presence try to command her.

Lintwo's head snapped around, her glare boring into a boy physically a few years younger than her. "Apologize," Lintwo commanded right back. Her presence seemed to tower even over the dragons for a brief second. The boy and a few others fainted.

Lintwo looked around, then took a deep breath. "He tried to command me," she said.

"She seems more like Death than you do," an older shade said to Woodrow.

"I have a few of Lindy's memories," Lintwo shrugged. That pressured the guests more than Lintwo's command.

A while later a buffet was set up, and a relaxed party began. The older shade sat next to Lintwo and extended a hand. "Maxeuis Landerall, speaker of the Duskglow conclave."

Lintwo rolled her eyes but shook the man's hand. "Lintwo Frostdottir Reaper." Lintwo used the name the school had adopted for her after the park incident. "So what is the Duskglow conclave? That sounds new."

"Duskglow has been an independent city for 112 years," Maxeuis said calmly.

"My knowledge of current history is a bit lacking for now, but that's what school is for, and you can think of me as a more specialized watcher," Lintwo answered Maxeuis's unasked questions.

"Specialized how?" Violet asked as she walked over with her daughter.

"I have a job to do that they were not built for. For now that's all I can say." Lintwo sighed before holding up a glass of juice. "To networking." Those nearby answered her toast.

Lintwo hopped off her seat. "I'm going to enjoy the party now." Lintwo walked toward where most of the young adults stood while holding Qilpee's hand.

"Done with your secret talks?" an elf asked.

Lintwo sighed. "Not even close, but I came to enjoy myself, not discuss any long-term plans."

Of the seven young adults at the party, five stayed together. Lintwo and Qilpeea spent the rest of the party eating and playing games with the young adult group while ignoring the three younger children a few feet away.

At the end of the party, Maxeuis met Lintwo at the gate. "By the way, is there anything I can do for you?"

"Do not make any statues of me or tell others about whatever you think I am," Lintwo said.

"I imagine Death would say much the same thing," Maxeuis replied.

Lintwo crossed her arms. "How about this: I need a space program for exploring past our solar system. You get your city to finance that, and I'll provide some technological know-how this world has not developed yet."

Maxeuis could not hide his manic grin. "That would be a true blessing for my people."

Lintwo glared at the old shade. "I will give spies a chance to steal that data, and a council of many nations will need to work together to assign the crew and supply the project. So how much your city can gain will be up to your people's skill and speed."

Maxeuis nodded. "We will not fail you."

"Fine, but if anyone starts acting like a zealot or fanatic obsessing over me, I will stop that behavior by any means necessary," Lintwo replied before getting into Woodrow's vehicle.

The ride back grew more dusty as the green manor disappeared over a particularly large sand dune. Stacy asked, "Did you really mean all of that?"

"I need to accelerate this planet's space program, so yes," Lintwo nearly snapped.

"That could give you a lot of power and influence," Woodrow said.

"I really am not looking forward to that." Lintwo grumbled, "I'm beginning to understand why World Spirits try to keep their distance from things and delegate tasks a lot."

School resumed after the one-week shutdown, then months passed. Qilpeea did not ask Lintwo about her bloodline, which was appreciated. Besides Samandrea and Qilpeea, the other students stayed away from Lintwo. Even the staff, if given the opportunity, gave her as wide a berth as they could.

Lintwo and Maxeuis kept in touch, talking about their joint project every few weeks.

Lintwo joined the school's cooking club with her friends. The club met once a week after school. One day after a slower than normal club, Lintwo sat with Samandrea and Qilpeea on the bus back home. The sun began to set, and the red sky was dimming to night. A few factory workers and dead-eyed office grunts sat scattered in clumps.

The bus shook to one side. Qilpeea, who had been half asleep, jolted awake. "Lin..." she called, but before the young dragon could finish her friends' names, the bus exploded in flames. Metal tore, and the bus was sheared in half.

The two jagged flaming halves skidded along the road, crashing into the late commuter traffic. Qilpeea reflexively tried to protect her friends but had only managed to hug Samandrea close, protecting her from the initial burst of flame. Smoke, fire, and screams filled the air.

Samandrea coughed. Her eyes stung from thick smoke, and the smell of burning flesh and oil filled her senses. Samandrea saw a chunk of the bus fall away as Lintwo pushed the jagged metal off herself.

Lintwo's own blood covered her. The deep gashes and burns on Lintwo's body began to heal at a visible rate. Lintwo did not feel pain, only adrenaline as her body prepared for combat. She was annoyed at herself for believing she could live a normal life for a time after the dryads' attempt on her life. Under all that was rage at whoever had targeted her because that seemed more likely than some random chance. It had been a slow day, after all.

Lintwo stood in the center of the chaos. She drew The End from within herself and cut a bullet shot at her head before sinking into the deep shadows produced from the flames, appearing behind the sniper who had shot her before stabbing him in the shoulder.

Lintwo snapped the rifle in half with one hand before dragging the human shooter to the edge of the rooftop he had been lying on. Lintwo held the man off the roof's edge above the burning street far below. "How many this time?" she asked.

"We are innumerable," the man spat.

"And the civilian casualties are just acceptable losses?" Lintwo demanded. The flashing lights of emergency personnel began to glint in the distance even as the plumes of smoke grew.

"Anything for your end. The empire's heirs will rise again," the man groaned.

Lintwo dropped the man. He screamed, but instead of hitting the pavement at terminal velocity, he fell into a shadow, only to fly out of Lintwo's shadow back into her hand over the road again. The man spit at Lintwo, who dodged it and kneed him hard in the gut, winding the man before slamming him onto the roof, knocking him out. Lintwo tied the man up with a spool of cabling and hung the man by his chest off the building. Lintwo tossed the rifle back onto the street and fell into her shadow again.

Lintwo appeared near Qilpeea, who was lending a shoulder to Samandrea. Lintwo took Samandrea's other side. Lintwo's wounds were fully healed but still a little sore. Lintwo looked around and called out to the shell-shocked servitors stumbling around, "Emergency services are coming from the city center. They should be here soon." Lintwo adjusted her friend's course as they navigated around debris.

Without another word a small line of people followed them to the edge of the wreckage.

"So much for the simple life," Lintwo replied.

"Thanks for the help," Samandrea coughed.

"Being near me almost got you killed again," Lintwo pointed out.

"This chaos will spread. You can't stop it, and I doubt it's about you being near. You may be the safest place in this world," Qilpeea said. Lintwo could only stare up into the sky, hoping that for the world's sake that was not the case. It was already taking all her willpower not to do something drastic.

The survivors were all transported to a hospital and questioned briefly while government personnel combed the scene. The sniper's body was found quickly. He was later identified as being in a revolutionary movement whose members believed they were descended from an empire that had once spanned the wasteland, ignoring that it was not an empire but more a warmongering kingdom and that, with a handful of exceptions, all that had called that kingdom home died with it.

4

Moving Forward

The next few weeks moved fast. Security in the city increased, checkpoints were set up on the streets, and even the school hired a few security guards. The group that had bombed the bus released a statement. They called themselves the Heirs of Derndell, and their statement claimed they were hunting their ancestral enemy to take back their birthright.

One night a knock sounded on Lintwo's door. Woodrow opened his door to find Samandrea, her mother, Qilpeea, and Violet standing outside in the cold. Bandages still covered half of Samandrea's face, but an uncharacteristic strength filled Samandrea's eyes. "We need to talk now."

"Ok, but..." Woodrow began to ask why.

Lintwo walked over. "Let them in, brother."

As the visitors were led in, Lintwo extended her hand to Samandrea's mother. "I'm Lintwo, something like a watcher."

"Kaitlaine, seer," the only visitor Lintwo did not know personally said.

"We still have some microwavable pizza, right?" Lintwo told Stacy.

"Ok, I'll be right back." Stacy nodded.

Once Stacy was fully entrenched, making a bigger dinner than planned, and the visitors were seated, Lintwo's gaze became cold. "Short version now, please."

"It's a long story," Kaitlaine said.

"Then give me the highlights," Lintwo pressed.

Samandrea shook. "There's going to be a war, bigger than any in a long time. A lot of cities will likely crumble."

Lintwo looked up at the ceiling. "And the delusional terrorists that targeted me are leading it, right?" She sighed.

"At first they will; after that I'm not sure. The future is never certain, but rarely this uncertain," Kaitlaine added as she hugged her shaking daughter.

"Well, shit." Lintwo grimaced. "Bro, I'm accelerating the schedule and moving to Duskglow."

Stacy chose that time to enter with food. "Already?"

"My friend's safety and the project come first, so yes," Lintwo sighed.

"When do we leave?" Violet asked.

"You know that's not what I meant by keeping you safe. Being close to me puts a target on your back," Lintwo said.

"I'm a dragon; we go where we want." Qilpeea replied.

"Eat first, and then we can leave." Woodrow smiled.

"So what's the plan?" Samandrea asked through a mouthful of scalding pizza before rushing to chug a bottle of water her mother had already prepared.

"You know I can't defend all of you, right?" Lintwo asked.

"Like Qilpeea said, I'm safest near you. So what will you do?" Samandrea scowled before going into a coughing fit. Kaitlaine gently patted her daughter's back.

"Turn Duskglow into a fortress, advance their technology, sell slightly worse plans to keep everyone honest, and build a spaceship able to travel past multiple solar systems." Lintwo shrugged as she enjoyed the pizza with more gusto and mess than her apparent age would imply.

"Either way, we should leave this city soon," Kaitlaine announced.

In his long life Woodrow had learned to trust advice from those close to Fate. Kaitlaine had a reputation as a powerful seer, which made her interpretation of possible futures reliable.

"Ok, we can leave tonight. Are you four coming, and what about your husbands?" Woodrow asked.

"Sam has to stay another week before he can transfer," Kaitlaine replied.

Violet shrugged. "Dragons don't always form long-term pairs."

Woodrow and Lintwo loaded up the all-terrain vehicle. Violet had a small surplus combat jeep all set with bags lashed to the top, while Kaitlaine's van was loaded with supplies. A few hours later the three vehicles left in the middle of the night.

Soon only Lintwo, Woodrow, Kaitlaine, and Violet were awake; the other three were too tired from their stress. Lintwo kept her eyes closed; she found an ability to sense things moving in darkness. It was an ability she would have to explore in depth, but for now it allowed her to perceive far more than her eyes could, even around corners.

The city streets were well lit, but the sidewalks, storefronts, and alleys were dark. They moved past the city center, which was all lights and tall glass buildings, which forced Lintwo to open her eyes, as her newly discovered sense was not useful when night was as bright as day. A few roundabouts later, dark brick buildings lined dim streets. Lintwo relaxed a little more as her shadow senses made themselves known again.

The way out of the city was easy; no border crossings were needed in this time of peace. The highway was mostly empty. Green trees and spare buildings dotted the side as the small convoy quickly moved along. A few cargo trucks were, for the most part, the only other vehicles on the highway so late.

They stopped around afternoon at a truck stop, ate brunch at the stop's diner, refilled gas, and slept for a while before resuming the trip.

"So do you have a contact number for Maxeuis?" Lintwo asked her brother.

"No," Woodrow replied. Lintwo raised an eyebrow. "I don't keep up to date on Lindy's followers," Woodrow explained.

Lintwo closed her eyes and faced the ceiling. "No problem. I've got a backup plan then, but when we get to the city, you need to look after the others for a while and stay together."

It was night when they arrived on the border of Duskglow. The border control staff looked through the IDs and passports of the travelers before letting them through. Lintwo felt an odd connection with the city of Duskglow. One of Lindy's vaguer memories informed Lintwo that this was likely because most of the city was populated by shades.

On a street filled with hotels, Lintwo got out of her brother's vehicle. "See you soon," Woodrow said as his sister slipped into a shadow. Stacy woke up when Woodrow started driving again. "She'll be fine," Woodrow explained.

Lintwo shifted from place to place, moving between dark corners and hidden spots. She was the shadows, and they were her. For hours she avoided car lights and lampposts. Lintwo slipped into a government tax office, and after finding the file room and shifting through the alphabetized system, Lintwo located Maxeuis's address. It was a manor near the center of the city.

Shifting from one dark corner to another, Lintwo eventually arrived at Maxeuis's manor. The manor was surrounded by a tall, fancy, and pointed wrought iron fence. The grounds were well lit by searchlights. Indeed, the center of the city was well lit to a pathological degree, almost as if powerful shades feared living in darkness.

The sculpted hedges did cast a few shadows. If anything, all the light made the few pools of darkness longer and deeper.

Lintwo kept out of sight of the walls and guards as she slipped from shadow to shadow. None of Maxeuis's guards were shades, and all held submachine guns with powerful flashlights attached under the barrel. The guards moved purposely but with little unison or enthusiasm. Exploitable gaps in their patterns were seized by Lintwo as she rolled and slinked through the few places where her connection to the shadows would not reach.

Maxeuis's security setup seemed built to counter someone with Lintwo's inherent skill set.

Lintwo found a window partly hidden by the shadow of a balcony one floor up. She swiftly forced it open, but a guard's flashlight swept over to the nook where the window sat. Lintwo almost shifted through the window into a small washroom before the light hit, but her feet went from being made of shadow to fleshy with cheap sneakers. Quickly Lintwo slinked out, knowing it was a matter of time before things got complicated. Her only chance of keeping things from getting difficult was finding Maxeuis and hashing out the deal she needed by any means necessary. Lintwo hoped the price Maxeuis got in the end did not blow up in the world's face too badly.

The halls were paneled in dark wood. Unlike outside, the lamps inside were not nearly as bright and were placed far enough apart that more darkness filled the manor. A few hallways led to the main reception areas and entryways, which were more thoroughly lit. A few shade guards with equipment of far better make patrolled, but not in enough numbers to be an issue for Lintwo.

Lintwo evaded the few guards she ran across by slipping into side rooms. She spotted a maid carrying a tray of coffee and cookies and slipped into the maid's shadow. Slowly the guards became more animated, but Lintwo was being carried along within the shadow of someone that should be in the manor.

The maid stopped at a second-floor office. She knocked on the door. "Sir, I have returned with your snacks."

Maxeuis's voice called from within the office, "Come in."

The office was covered in carpet, tapestries, and book-shelves stuffed with old leather-bound tomes. Lintwo slipped into the shadow of the open door. Once the maid left and shut the door, light hit Lintwo's hiding spot, revealing her.

Maxeuis dipped a cookie into his coffee. "Are you why my guards are on high alert?"

Lintwo crossed her arms. "That's right. I have it on good authority life is going to get much more interesting."

"And you need something else from me." Maxeuis nodded somberly.

Lintwo chuckled; she could feel Maxeuis's fear. "We need to make a deal; I will not ask for anything for free."

"What's your proposal?" Maxeuis asked.

"You give me control of the space program's R&D depart-ment and I'll help develop other advanced projects. You will need far better defenses and farms," Lindy replied.

Maxeuis knew it was not as simple as his guest put it. "That's very generous. Why the urgency?"

Lintwo smiled. "The coming war will be difficult."

"What war?" Maxeuis asked.

Lintwo's expression fell. "Some zealots who think any-thing related to Death herself must be destroyed and claim their ancestors survived Death's wrath. Primal chaos will more than likely once again take hold."

"I suppose I'll need to help you settle into my city and get you more involved in the R&D process." Maxeuis sighed. On the surface the deal worked better for him, but the threat that the new terrorist group and Lintwo herself posed forced his hand.

"I am planning to live here with a few others, but if you do provide special treatment, try to not make it too overt." Lintwo nodded as she walked next to Maxeuis and opened a window. "Do you need anything else right now?" she asked.

"No, give me a few weeks to set things up and analyze this threat, and I'll get back to you somehow," Maxeuis replied, knowing that he would need to deal with a lot more paperwork directly for a while.

When Maxeuis opened his eyes, Lintwo was already gone, having shifted into the shadows on the roof and then back to the street.

It took a few weeks for Lintwo and company to get settled in. The adults' work visas were approved quickly. Kaitlaine's husband, Sam, arrived two weeks into their relocation.

School began again. Lintwo attended, if only to keep a heathier mental balance. A lot of humans and orcs, plus a handful of shades, attended. Lintwo kept quiet in her classes, stepping in only when Qilpeea or Samandrea got bullied. Samandrea tried to hide near Lintwo, and Qilpeea naturally became the voice of their little group. The school the three friends attended was in a relatively safe neighborhood. It had once been well maintained before most of its taxpayer money was shifted to newer schools in nicer areas that were almost exclusively populated by shades.

A group of boys began to give Samandrea a hard time. They did not stop even after Lintwo tripped them in the halls each time using her magic. The group's leader was a human named Tomless.

Lintwo found the abandoned tollbooth the boys hung out in after school. One Friday she arrived at the booth and knocked on its door. "Hey, stop messing with my friends," Lintwo demanded of the five boys.

"No," Tomless replied flatly.

"That's not how this works. You fools have made my friends sad. You have two choices: never talk to my friends again or tell me why right now, and maybe I won't beat the stuffing out of you," Lintwo demanded.

"We don't need to tell you anything," Tomless's biggest friend said.

Lintwo poked the boy in the chest; she knew his name was Jeffrin and that he hated it. "Jeff, can I call you Jeff? Please shut the fuck up."

The big boy swung at Lintwo. She shifted into the shadows for a few seconds, and Jeffrin's fist passed through her. Lintwo grabbed the boy's arm and twisted it. "Tom, can I call you Tom? Why are you making Samandrea's life hard?"

"I like her, all right? Happy?" Tomless admitted.

The shadows around them departed. "Not completely, but that's good enough for now. Consider this your last warning to be nice to her." With that, Lintwo walked away.

Tomless worked up the courage to yell after Lintwo. "Hey, what's a shade mage doing in our school?"

Lintwo laughed. "Both my parents were technically human." Her mirth was the mirror image of Lindy as it echoed from the shadows eerily.

A month after arriving, the same maid Lintwo had used to sneak into Maxeuis's office arrived at Woodrow's door.

"I need to pick up something from a Miss Reaper?" the maid asked.

"Come in, I'll call her," Woodrow offered.

"I'll stay here," the maid said.

Woodrow shrugged. "Sis, someone is here to see you," he called out.

When the maid saw Lintwo, she did a double take. "I think I have the wrong house."

"Did Max send you?" Lintwo asked.

The maid seemed insulted on her employer's behalf. "Lord Maxeuis sent me."

"Right, not so loud." Lintwo rolled her eyes before grabbing two napkins and a pen. She spread the napkins out and wrote on them furiously. Soon after, Lintwo handed the napkins to the maid. "Deliver these directly to Maxeuis. Do not smudge them." The maid took the napkins carefully, but she still seemed confused. The maid's shadow rose up and tapped her on the shoulder. "The less you know, the better," Lintwo explained, thankful that someone seemingly loyal and clueless was the courier. Once the maid realized Lintwo was not what she seemed, the maid turned to flee.

"I do have one question before you run off." Lintwo whispered, but the maid stopped as if she had been struck. Lintwo could see the fear in the servant's eyes. "You know my name. It's only fair I know yours."

"Shafon Filsevon," the maid replied.

Lintwo was beginning to realize she likely was auto-translating most words. "Cool, I guess I'll see you next time," Lintwo said before closing the door.

"What did you give her?" Woodrow asked.

"Plans for a power generator and an automated fabrication CPU," Lintwo said.

Woodrow crossed his arms. "You already have a deal in the works, don't you?"

Lintwo sat down and went back to enjoying lunch. "I told you that was the plan."

For the rest of the year tension built, a few more banks were robbed than the year before, a handful of news outlets slowly became more xenophobic, and a large number of politicians began trying to enact isolationist policies. It was apparent to all who tried to see that something big was happening on the world stage, but no one on the ground floor looking up knew what the asses on the thrones saw.

As fear grew, the local shades became more intolerant of non-shades. The feeling was swiftly reciprocated. Not all other city-states or bigger nations were so lucky to have the tension remain simmering under the slick surface veneer of normalcy. Some nations' fears and hatred boiled over, filling the streets with blood and more rage that seeped into other nations.

Maxeuis closed his city-state's borders and began to censor the news even more than before. Each month Lintwo would provide more manufacturing techniques and a few weapon diagrams and some formulas for alloys. Some of those alloys and techniques went into building a wall all around Dusk-glow.

Lintwo's school life got more difficult. Shades could feel their creator's presence on her, even if most had no idea why the shades showed Lintwo respect and deference. All the shades felt that they should never make Lintwo truly angry, and that terrified the more introspective ones. Maxeuis had to wave off complaints and questions other shades had about Lintwo.

Most people Lintwo lived around were not shades and were on the poor side, something that local government seemed to take steps to keep as the norm. Lintwo became feared and hated by almost all the non-shades around her. The school even did a surprise medical check on its students, where it was discovered that Lintwo was human, which seemed to freak out the staff even more. The school's governing board was replaced the next day, which did not help the growing paranoia directed at Lintwo, which became even greater when the shades in the local police force that investigated were more respectful of Lintwo than their own captain, which many non-shades saw.

Most of the more advanced blueprints Lintwo provided to Maxeuis required the power generator plans she had handed over. The generator used fission with crystallized magic and the rocks from the anti-magic pit in her home city to produce magic power. It was Lintwo's way of getting the generators built so her own plans of building a starship could be accelerated.

The first spies to steal a copy of Lintwo's blueprints stole plans for a greenhouse that required the magic fission generator for some of its more innovative tech.

During the week of school vacation, a minor event in the grand scheme of things shifted the course of history.

Lintwo was sitting at a park with summer vacation homework. Tomless, his crew of friends, Qilpeea, Samandrea, and around 50 adult humans crowded the park. The adults all had improvised weapons. Without looking up, Lintwo asked, "Qilpeea, Samandrea, are they with you?"

"Get out of our city, monster," one of the bigger humans snapped.

"Dad?" Tomless asked.

Lintwo looked into Qilpeea and Samandreas's eyes. "What do you two want?"

"You should not be here," Samandrea replied.

"Is that a prophecy or your personal feelings?" Lintwo prodded.

"You are just two different people; please leave," Samandrea said.

"And you are just following her whims?" Lintwo asked Qilpeea. The adults in the park felt afraid for their lives as Lintwo kept talking. It was hard for them to talk, and that made the mob even angrier and justified the hate they felt for Lintwo by her association with the shades.

"I trust her," Qilpeea said.

Lintwo smiled; it was eerily wide and just as hollow. "Fine, then plan D it is."

Samandrea dropped to the ground shrieking, "No, not that! Why did things change so drastically?"

All hell broke loose. Qilpeea turned to her friend, but before she could ask, Tomless rushed to Samandrea's side. Lintwo stood up and flowed around three adults who tried to hit her with clubs.

Lintwo knelt before Samandrea. "The most likely fate can be overturned sometimes by just one careless action." A club impacted the back of Lintwo's head. Blood dripped down Lintwo's face as she held Samandrea's gaze for a fraction of a second; it may well have been a millennium.

Lintwo stood up. Her wound had already begun to heal. "Now will I be allowed to walk away unharmed, or will we do this the hard way?" Lintwo's voice echoed from every shadow for blocks in every direction.

The adults had paused after Lintwo began to bleed, but as one they chose not to flee but to fight. Lintwo's face fell; each adult's shadow lengthened out of each shadow came an inky featureless form that restrained the adults. "You are a watcher," one of the older adults hissed.

"Oh, I'm more than that. Did Samandrea not mention my real name, which may as well be Lintwo Reaper?" Lintwo sneered as the shadows broke each adult's dominant arm.

"So the Planes Walker cell failed to kill you," another adult snapped.

Lintwo raised an eyebrow, finding her foe's lack of information control short-sighted. "Good to know."

"We will not bow to Death," a few of the humans yelled as they fought their bonds.

Lintwo rolled her eyes. "There are far worse things than my parents," she said as she walked out of the park, trying to look in control as something inside broke.

Lintwo walked home. Stacy met her in the kitchen. "How was your day?" Stacy began, but upon seeing Lintwo's face, she knew something was wrong. "What happened?" Stacy asked as she walked over.

"My brother is out?" Lintwo asked. Stacy tried to make sense of what was going on and did not answer, so Lintwo went on, "You two need to move out of this city-state and keep your heads down." Lintwo began to grab bags and stuff her brother's clothes and other supplies inside.

"Why?" Stacy managed to ask. She had never seen Lintwo so frantic.

"Because this city is a target and the unrest is boiling over." Lintwo replied hurriedly. She tossed Stacy a few empty bags. "Get packed up; chances are this will get bad soon. To those that don't know any better, I seem like a shade, and to those that know too much, I seem like a watcher. Being near me makes you a target."

"That's not right. We should stay with you." Stacy said,

"I cannot guarantee your safety even with Woodrow and me. So you need to leave," Lintwo pressed.

The door was knocked down, and Woodrow stumbled in. His clothes were ripped, and he had some bruises. Lintwo tossed the bags she filled to him. "Get her out of the city and lay low."

"And leave you here?" Woodrow asked. Stacy was spooked but ran over to Woodrow and checked him over.

"My war starts here. You have someone to protect. Our travel buddies betrayed us. I'm kind of jealous of you, honestly," Lintwo explained, but could not keep her voice neutral.

Woodrow looked at his sister. She was afraid and alone but was trying to keep to a mission that was bigger than any one mortal should ever need to shoulder. "You could run," Woodrow said.

Lintwo shook her head. "I can end this somehow."

A few hours later Woodrow and Stacy were out of the city, safe. Riots had begun, and Lintwo moved to find Maxeuis. The start of a war had caught her on the back foot, but Lintwo swore she would find a way to end it.

Small groups of armed humans moved around the poorer district. Lintwo snuck around scattered mobs and a line of riot personnel that cut off half the city. The riot teams' deployments were a little messy as they tried to form the metaphorical line in the sand the city leaders desired, plus getting all personnel up and on active duty took time they didn't have. The center of the city was almost deserted save for a few security guards on high alert.

Lintwo slipped up to a rooftop and shifted from one roof's shadow to another until she was across from the window to Maxeuis's study. The window was slightly ajar. Lintwo shifted into the room. Maxeuis and two other shades sat in the study. They leapt up when Lintwo appeared in the room and sat on the room's sole desk. "It's getting bad out there. Already had to relocate my family, and the rioters may have at least a dragon or two."

Maxeuis introduced them. "This is Lintwo. She is a very talented ally. My colleagues Mildilta Shadowsong, chief of our R&D, and Azole Xeneder, the city's chief of security."

"How did they get two dragons?" Azole demanded. Lintwo decided she liked the chief of security, as he did not question the apparent child before him after his boss said she was ok. Although like all shades, Azole felt deep in his subconscious that Lintwo was someone to be obeyed.

"I thought they were my friends. More fool me." Lintwo shrugged, still trying to drown that feeling of betrayal as swiftly as possible.

"Did you cause the riot?" Maxeuis asked.

Lintwo rolled her eyes and made a show of being disappointed, taking shelter in the act. "You did, this city did. Granted, I'm sure someone or some group of someones used the inequality here to rouse the people here to riot, but this makes them victims even more."

Azole rubbed his eyes. "We missed that."

Lintwo stamped her feet. The shadows in the room shifted for a few seconds, and the adults before her cowered. "How!" Lintwo demanded. She ripped the window from its hinges as a few sporadic gunshots echoed through the silent night before all hell broke loose outside. Fires and automatic weapons fire followed. "How do you miss the spark for that! How do you drop the ball for any real kind of olive branch or human decency that hard?"

"We could not have known," Mildilta sputtered.

"What was the highest priority order Lindy Shrew ever gave your kind?" Lintwo demanded, her voice carried high above the sounds of distant automatic weapons.

"To help our kind," Mildilta said with some feeling.

"To. Play. Nice." Lintwo enunciated slowly, making each word hit like a hammer.

"Do you have a way to fix this?" Maxeuis demanded.

"Play nice with others and let me try to save those who don't want to fight but are caught in that warzone you let happen," Lintwo replied.

5

A Loss of Innocence

Maxeuis looked at his main two followers. Neither Mildilta nor Azole had a good argument against Lintwo's demand. If the teenager was their equal or out-ranked them on the cosmic scale of things, then they had no arguments after being called out so thoroughly, besides getting emotional, which seemed like a dangerous choice.

"I'll help you find a uniform and any gear you need," Azole offered.

"Lead the way, Maxeuis. I don't want any noncombatants harmed. We can't take back this mess, but we can try to fix what we can," Lintwo said as she left the room. Maxeuis ran ideas for damage control, all the while knowing that staying on Lintwo's good side might be the only way his city could survive as an independent state.

Azole led Lintwo through fine wood-paneled halls to a grand staircase. An old bolt-action rifle rested in a display cabinet. "Any issues if I take that?" Lintwo asked.

Azole looked at the display's plaque. "I don't have any reason to refuse. Some of our weapons still use this ammo, but I'd suggest you get some of the armory staff to look it over."

Azole led Lintwo to an airlock door under the grand stairway that led to a large metal-walled basement lit by fluorescent blue lights. Azole ignored the reception and guard desk. Just past that, a team of ten people in heavy riot gear were assembling and getting ready to move out. A female shade led them, but most of the unit was made up of humans, goblins, cat folk, and one ogre. "Officer Latool, I'm putting you and your team on search and rescue detail under command of this advisor." Azole realized he did not know how to address Lintwo or what her full name was and looked down at Lintwo, who was getting many conflicting looks.

"My full name should be Lintwo Reaper. You don't need to know anything else besides that. We will need a few non-lethal weapons and a lot of lethal ones." Lintwo grinned; she chose to put off her fears and regrets for another time. Lintwo handed Azole the bolt-action rifle. "I'll need a hair-trigger and a holographic sight on this and a few hundred rounds and a few armor-piercing and incendiary rounds if you have them. I'll get Officer Latool to help me with the rest of my gear."

Azole took the weapon. Normally he would resist, but time was of the essence, and he knew in his bones that pissing off Lintwo was a bad idea. "All right, Latool, see that Miss Reaper gets geared up, and if you need to request anything from the armory for her or your team, call them and I'll rubber-stamp it." Azole walked briskly away, having maintained some dignity as a superior officer.

Lintwo looked over the team who had not yet decided what to think of her. "You lot are going to need some shock batons now. Any chance I can get a uniform, chest plate, boots, and baton in my size?" Lintwo asked.

Lintwo was quickly provided her gear from the sets usually used by the goblins. Lintwo made sure her gear had no rank insignia. Latool handed Lintwo a hair tie, earpiece, and throat microphone. Maxeuis returned soon after Lintwo took the rifle and tested the action, then tossed most of the five boxes of ammo she was given into her shadow. The team's radio frequency was set to be used only by them and the main HQ.

Latool split a case of zip ties with the team as they walked out of the armory with Lintwo in the lead. At the gates, Lintwo closed her eyes, slowed her breathing, and focused. All movement in the city flowed into her mind. Blood dripped from Lintwo's eyes and nose from the info overload. When she opened her eyes, Lintwo pointed to a street. "We are going that way. Keep close, but don't bunch up." Then she ran off with her team hot on her heels.

The group moved through a street, then an alley, and out to another street where a flipped patrol car burned. Two battered patrolmen were being dragged from the vehicle by a mob of humans, elves, and goblins united in attacking symbols of local authority. A few pipes, a shotgun, and a few handguns were raised when Lintwo broke out into the road. "Weapons down now," she yelled out as she raised her own.

A bullet fired from the mob would have taken Lintwo's ear if she had not been moving low and taking care to shift the direction of her body often, keeping one shoulder and her side facing the guns. More of the mob raised their guns. The violence and confidence of being in a mob had the mob make a choice as one. Lintwo whispered into her throat mike, "Clear the street by any means necessary."

Lintwo raised her gun and put an incendiary round right in the chest of an elf holding the mob's only shotgun. Lintwo's team opened up with their carbines; the street was cleared out quickly. After a quick scan of the street, Lintwo checked the two wounded officers' vitals. One opened his eyes. "I'm sending you back to HQ to make a report ASAP," she ordered before the patrolman sank into the long shadows and appeared beside the armory. Lintwo left the other officer, as he was already in Death's realm. She avoided looking into the eyes of the dead and hardened her heart. It was going to be a long night.

The team walked on. Latool made a note of each unsecured alley, overrun barricade, and unguarded intersection, calling each one into HQ.

They ran into a few civilians fleeing the chaos and tied them up. Lintwo sent them to an emergency detention block Latool was given the coordinates for.

The firefights increased in number and intensity as they got closer to the city's edge and the more time went on.

A small group of civilians surrendered to Lintwo and company, but one set off a pipe bomb when Latool went to zip-tie his hands. Lintwo let a bubble of shadow envelop the man and absorb the shards caused by the explosion. Some heat still leaked from the bubble. After Lintwo was sure the man was fading fast, she thrust her hand into a shadow darkening a wall and had her arm and a shard of glass slit the man's throat from the exit portal before dissipating the shadow bubble. No one said anything for the next few blocks.

Unarmed civilians rushed past down broken streets. Most storefronts had been fully looted in the short time of the insurgency's flare-up.

Lintwo came upon a group of children even younger than she appeared looting a bread stall. "Take what you can, then flee," was Lintwo's ultimatum to the children. A gun clicked behind her. Lintwo swirled around to see a man leveling a revolver at her. Normally Lintwo would dodge, but the children were behind her. Lintwo raised her rifle, but before she could draw a bead, three shots were fired.

Latool stood in front of Lintwo. The shade was hit twice, once in the body armor and once in the leg. The gunman had been shot in the throat by Latool and was bleeding out, gurgling across the street.

Lintwo checked Latool over. The bullet to the leg had hit an artery and Latool was fading fast. "I'm not losing anyone else today," Lintwo said as she slapped her face. "Stay awake for a few more seconds. This will hurt."

Lintwo filled Latool with the same kind of magic that had created the first shades. It was far weaker, but unlike Lintwo's namesake, there was only one target this time.

Latool's body rebuilt itself. Her entire body snapped in many places as things reknitted and grew stronger. After she was done, Lintwo looked up at her team and found the children had run off. "Take her back. I'll handle the rest alone,"

Lintwo said. Her eyes were the darkest things in the unlit street.

"But our orders…" one of the squad began.

"Have been given, so go," Lintwo snapped as she stood up and double-checked her ammo. Lintwo pocketed the re-volver that had almost wounded her and stalked off to the city's edge.

By now Maxeuis's forces had begun to move forward, sweeping street by street, alleyway by alleyway. For the most part, their rules of engagement were the same as Lintwo's, which she appreciated.

Lintwo moved towards the enemy-controlled center, ig-noring any rebels that were not moving into areas she had al-ready swept.

Samandrea, Kaitlaines, Sam, Qilpeea, Violet, and Tomless were among the few still in the HQ. Twenty-five of the adults Samandrea had led to Lintwo were present as well. A tall man in austere robes stood in the middle of the command center, but he seemed removed from the action and in the center of it at the same time.

The rebel HQ was a series of tents set up outside a ruined church. Radios and a snack bar were set up with some kind of plan.

Lintwo rolled her eyes at the pathetic guard detail. She fixed the rifle with The End. The light-eating, shape-changing knife took the form of a short bayonet this time.

Lintwo appeared in a flash of darkness behind the austere man, her bayonet already in his spine. As the man fell gasping, Lintwo fired one shot from her revolver into his head. Lintwo looked around. The enemy HQ was still in panic when Lintwo saw Samandrea panicking. Her rage lessened, and the unnatural darkness filling the HQ lashed out, branding those who remained and taking their magic. None of the survivors in that HQ would ever be able to use any magic, including Samandrea, who would never again be able to tell what the future might bring. Interestingly, Lintwo felt that Fate had not attempted to protect Samandrea's ability at all. "I'm sorry," Lintwo whispered, knowing that by not killing them, some, like Samandrea, would risk madness as they got used to being cut off from all magic, but Lintwo could not bring herself to create more corpses that night, and so she slid into the shadows, stepping back near Maxeuis's HQ.

The rest of the night was semi-organized chaos. After the riots, many were without homes. Those who did not take up arms were allowed to stay if they so chose. The ones who fought against the city but lived either fled or were executed. The international community would have normally had some harsh words if many other mini revolutions had not sprung up all around the world at the same time. The cells that rose up were not well coordinated, and many were opportunistic militaristic groups or even deniable government assets.

Three cells did take over one city each, and so the wars raged on. Duskglow closed its borders; no one entered and no one left. Walls were slowly erected over the next few years. At year five of the war, the wall around Duskglow was completed. Mildilta stepped down as head of research and development, and Lintwo took her place. Maxeuis officially became the leader of Duskglow for the duration of the global conflict using emergency protocols. Lintwo made Cinithea Latool her chief bodyguard.

The next few years Maxeuis tried to get Lintwo to develop weapons, communication, and farming tech, but Lintwo was unable to get a budget for her personal mission of building a large spacecraft. To get around the railroading red tape, Lintwo often had to submit projects that overlapped with her own mission. Even then, the budget she was given would not cover her world's first interstellar starship.

6

No Step Back

Twenty more years of war passed as Lintwo worked as the head of R&D for the Duskglow city-state. The fighting began to die down after many populations had been decimated, including those born during the war who later took up arms. Ironically, it was not lack of will that stopped the fighting, but the lack of bodies to toss into the meat grinder that was war.

The cities of Fallenrest, Aglessea, and Caldrenhime had stayed in the hands of human zealots with the dogma of hating Death herself.

As the rest of the world's governments began to realize how worn down they had become, the city of Caldrenhime launched a salvo of rockets into all the cities around it, rockets Lintwo had developed and Duskglow had sold. The city leaders of Duskglow had tried to be neutral by selling weapons to all sides and not sending their troops out of the walls.

One night Lintwo sat at a desk angrily rereading an email. The R&D branch's board of directors had held a vote of no confidence in Lintwo's leadership and appointed a replacement, all without telling her about the vote. The only reason Lintwo learned so early was the R&D branches tried to repossess her three private labs with Maxeuis's support.

Maxeuis's term as emergency head of Duskglow was almost up as the war wound down, so he had begun to try to play all sides and take Lintwo's political clout down a few notches.

Lintwo read for a third time Maxeuis's overly polite request that she give up all her personal holdings. Lintwo spun in her chair and looked at Cinithea, who stood behind her employer and friend. Neither male nor female nor Lintwo had seemed to age in the twenty years they had worked together. "Pack it up. We're going to war," Lintwo growled.

"Is that wise, ma'am?" Cinithea asked with a raised eyebrow and good humor.

"It will make my former ally panic, so it's worth it. It won't take more than a week anyway. The automated defenses have more than enough ammo for that time frame," Lintwo grumbled.

Lintwo and Cinithea left the city that night. Maxeuis had lifted travel bans for a few merchants that year, and Lintwo was still one of those.

They kept driving over two days with a few breaks in the direction of the most concentrated and high numbers of deaths Lintwo could feel. They arrived at a once flat field that was now covered in more craters and diversions than even the bodies, and there were a lot of bodies. Some were even alive.

Around two-thirds of the corpses wore Caldrenhime insignia. "Now to find a few artillery systems," Lintwo said as she jumped out of their vehicle.

"And do what?" Cinithea asked.

"Cripple as many of the city's import/export hubs as possible with as many different nations' artillery as we can." Lintwo shrugged.

"That is highly illegal, ma'am," Cinithea pointed out as she walked behind Lintwo into the war zone.

"I know it is, so let's try to confuse things as much as possible," Lintwo nodded.

The first battery was simple enough to find. Lintwo raised a few armies' worth of undead from shallow mass graves, and they took out most of the artillery crews from behind but allowed the few that ran to flee. For the next half hour, as soon as all the coordinates were locked and a countdown was set, Lintwo and Cinithea frantically made the ten or so artillery batteries fire at five different nations. Lintwo, her growing undead hoard, and Cinithea left to hunt down a new battery from a different faction. When Lintwo found any weapons from Duskglow on the battlefield, she subtly broke them so that they could not be reused without an involved repair job. Randomly, Lintwo would recalibrate a weapon not from Duskglow to work just a bit better than it had before.

Some batteries were still manned by the living. Some were not by the time Lintwo arrived, but each casualty added to her horde. Lintwo could only hope that the damage to each nation's infrastructure would cause their civilians to categorically refuse to support the war when their few remaining luxury and other comfort items disappeared from the markets. If each nation blamed the other, then maybe they would agree to a ceasefire at least.

That night only Lintwo, Cinithea, and the horde remained on the battlefield. Lintwo let her undead horde cease to animate.

Other battles still went on, so Lintwo and Cinithea visited three more over the next two days and repeated the process.

A few road signs proclaiming an upcoming peace treaty began to litter the roadway. Lintwo chose to drive back to Duskglow.

Near the city fires, Lintwo sighed and got out of her car.

Cinithea and Lintwo stalked closer to Duskglow only to see a battalion from Caldrenhime besieging Duskglow's walls. Lintwo sensed that she had removed the ability for magic among the attackers, which included her old friends.

"No matter what, stay out of this fight," Lintwo ordered.

"But I can…" Cinithea began.

Lintwo shook her head firmly, cutting off her friend. "One more body will not change things, so stay back." Lintwo knew this was personal. Her inherited experience had one way to handle this, and that way was best solo.

Lintwo unscrewed The End from its bayonet mount; her knife shifted into a long dagger. Lintwo and her rifle sank into her shadow, only for Lintwo, dagger in hand, to jump out in the midst of the enemy battalion, having traveled half a mile in seconds.

Before the battalion members knew that they were trapped in their own camp with Lintwo, ten of their one hundred members were dead.

A few sporadic wild shots were fired, but Lintwo moved in such a way that friendly fire was not a possibility, but a foregone conclusion. Fifteen more died from friendly fire before Lintwo bobbed and wove around the camp, reaping five more lives on the circuit.

Samandrea walked out of a tent, her eyes mad, as she threw open her hands and laughed. "I know you have come. We have conquered Death in spite of your curse. Come out and meet your end."

Lintwo sprang out from behind a pile of shells and stabbed a man in the throat as the new victim sputtered and died. Lintwo held up her blade. "My knife is The End." Lintwo made a spine made from the darkness of the dimming day spear through Samandrea's left leg. Samandrea fell to the ground, her left leg lost below the knee, but the energy required to push past her old friend's unforeseen level of magic resistance was difficult even for Lintwo. Any normal mage would have had their direct spells stopped cold.

The battalion of hardened and lavishly talked-up elites gawked at their leader being struck down by magic, as it was the first time Samandrea had been wounded in this way. "The hard way it is, then." Lintwo found the curses she had planted so many years before and pulled at the threads of power she had left behind. Twenty-five battalion members were pulled apart, unraveling like meaty yarn. The rest of the attackers were normal humans and surrendered at the horrifying sight.

Lintwo tied the hands of her prisoners and walked them up to the gates, where Maxeuis and a few officers stood. "You are back," he said. "Thank you for the assistance, but we really need to talk now."

Lintwo used her inherited power over the shades to order Maxeuis, "Tell me the truth. When are you planning to help me complete my project?"

Maxeuis answered against his will. "No, I don't need you anymore."

"Then die," Lintwo commanded.

Maxeuis turned on one of the officers, took the man's sidearm, and blew his own brains out.

Lintwo shook her head, too numb and upset to pay anyone a thought. "I'm taking back the labs until my project is done. The prisoners are yours."

Lintwo and Cinithea walked back into Duskglow. Once back in one of her personal underground lab fortresses, Lintwo remotely took over all of Duskglow's automated production network.

A few days later a peace deal was signed by all the world's nations. It was decided that the entire populations of Fallenrest, Aglessea, and Caldrenhime were to be turned over to Lintwo as labor. In return, Duskglow would give the other nations technical assistance. Every nation had been bled nearly dry of its manpower and other supplies. At most, the world had one big battle before all of civilization burned out, as there were just enough big guns left for that. The leaders of Fallenrest, Aglessea, and Caldrenhime knew their peoples' only hope for survival was their third greatest enemy, Lintwo's benevolence, Death herself being the worst foe to those cities and Woodrow the second because of his parentage and nothing else.

Lintwo was called to speak to the interim council in charge of Duskglow. The niceties were skipped the moment Lintwo walked into the council chamber, which was filled with heavily armed guards. "You have yet to return your three private labs," a council member pointed out.

"You have your production facilities back as agreed. Why should I give up my personal labs?" Lintwo asked calmly.

"Because your three labs have all the blueprints we need to fulfill the obligations in the treaty," a councilwoman raged.

Lintwo rolled her eyes. "And what will you pay me for my labs? They are my land."

"We have no money to give, and we can just take the land," a councilman said while suppressing his own fear and rage.

Lintwo crossed her arms. "I dare you to try to take what's mine. Give me resources worth the labs."

"Like what?" the chairman asked.

"The walls. It's not like you need them now. You don't fulfill the terms, and the world burns, or you do, and no one can fight for a while." Lintwo smirked.

"Fine," the chairman grumbled.

Lintwo left the meeting room, done with the greed of the world. Her labs were unsealed, but only one computer with the public blueprints she had helped develop remained within. The wall disappeared a few nights later, with no one in the city quite sure how.

After a few days of furious planning, Lintwo worked out how and where to move three cities' worth of displaced people. Lexi arrived at the camp Lintwo had created just outside of Duskglow's city limits. "You really had us on edge for a while."

Lintwo shoved a large pile of papers into Lexis's hands. "I need you to help Cinithea teach what's in that packet to a few thousand people who I can use as instructors."

Lexi looked at Lintwo for a while as Lintwo went back to poring over documents and jotting down notes and plans. Lexi turned her eyes from Lintwo and skimmed the papers she was still holding. Lexi had to reread the plans a few times. "You want us to teach people how to use a space suit and build, in space, a spaceship the size of many cities?"

"Well, they can't stay here. I've already taken Duskglow's walls plus the entirety of Fallenrest, Aglessea, and Caldrenhime," Lintwo replied calmly.

"Will that be enough?" Lexi asked.

"I don't know yet, but those refugees are my fault and my responsibility," Lintwo huffed.

Lexi sighed. "Just get some sleep once in a while," she said, before leaving to find Cinithea.

Days later at her mother's old city, near where three young, now separated friends had met years before, Lintwo stood at a train station. The mostly defunct yard and a few blocks around were filled with three cities' worth of scapegoats. The trains left with the tired and scared masses to the wasteland, where a large camp city was being created.

The next few months were a true logistical nightmare. Building walls and factories around the tent city was hard enough, but getting food for three cities' worth of displaced people was a daunting task.

Nothing really lived or grew in the wasteland. There was an old train station near the tent city from a failed past attempt to build a town. Lintwo, however, knew what few others remembered, and that was that an underground complex once used as part of a hero academy long ago sat just under the land. They blew through the food stores that had been kept in Fallenrest, Aglessea, and Caldrenhime, cities that Lintwo had managed to stuff into her shadow and part of Frost's realm, but the food had been put to good use as teams dug through the sand and bedrock to the entrance to an ancient complex where Lintwo hoped they could piece together farms.

Lintwo and a few of the diggers entered the ancient ruin that faded letters had once proudly informed all to be Hero Academy number 3.

Flashlights lit what magic had once lit back when spells had been common. Dust and petrified wooden furniture sat on each level. Some dull crystals that had once been magical and sand that had once been glass were scattered about. At the complex's ninth level was a huge and dim but faintly glowing crystal. "Would you look at that?" Lintwo smirked as she poked around the defunct magical power generator.

The diggers still did not trust Lintwo, but most understood that their former enemy was their one shot to live well, and that meant leaving their home world behind. Few fully believed Lintwo could get them off-world, but all knew that the nations of the world would never be kind to them, at least for many generations, if ever.

Stone planters filled all but the last level of the underground complex. Water was produced by a few advocates of Water. The food had almost run out when the first crops were ready to harvest.

While the first crops were being tended, Lintwo had been hard at work getting most of the adult population trained in using a spacesuit and setting up a plan to start building their colony ship in space. A few prefab buildings that would be used as the base of the ship were constructed while a few rocket ships and launchpads were created. The workers turned chunks of their own cities into the very things that would be part of their new home, which helped with morale.

Years rolled by, launch pads were built, and rocket ships were sent up to the very edge of the planet's gravity well, each ship transporting supplies and people. The only two good things about the wasteland were that it was hard to take and hold territory deep into the wasteland and that it was nearly all free real estate, meaning the log runways the rockets needed were easy to make.

Of the things that worried Lintwo on a nearly daily basis, most had to do with the outside, the main one being the few oil wells and iron deposits her city had found and begun to tap. The wasteland may have been very hard on all lifeforms but had other untapped resources. They had even found a small uranium deposit, which Lintwo had immediately ordered buried and removed from all records.

There were a few survivors of the group Lintwo had cursed, Qilpeea among them, as well as a few children of those who had inherited the curse. Qilpeea had kept the cursed ones from dealing with Lintwo.

As the colony ship took shape in orbit around their home world, the process of moving more and more people to the ship to live there and help complete it progressed at a steady pace. At the same time, the other nations of the world began to have their greed outweigh their caution, as infrastructure was fixed and birth rates soared, exceeding the food supplies needed for a healthy civilization.

Twenty years into constructing the colony ship, the main power generator was completed and the ship's onboard farms had a regular yield nearly double the first estimate. Over half of the exiles lived in space at this point, unified by their distrust of the rest of the world.

Lintwo set out to look over the generator and farms in a cleanroom near a dusty runway. She pulled on a spacesuit with practiced ease. Stepping out on a stretch of heavily compacted dust, she walked a short way across the wasteland to a large shuttle just as its refueling and takeoff processes were being finished.

Lexi met Lintwo at the ship's hatch. "I'll have that food tally ready for when you get back," Lexi promised.

"Good to hear. See you soon." Lintwo nodded, and without a backwards glance, she scampered into the shuttle while Lexi held the ladder.

"Let's go hit a bar when you get back," Lexi called out.

Lintwo double-checked her restraint harness and mumbled "Sure" before closing the door.

Soon the shuttle rumbled to life, and began its takeoff by shooting across the wasteland before taking to the sky in a gentle curve upwards, rocking straight up into the stratosphere. Lintwo hummed along with the engines as she looked over even more documents that needed to be approved by her (or not) by the end of the day.

Lintwo glanced out the shuttle's window after the shuttle exited her home world's atmosphere. No matter how many times she had seen it, looking down at her world from just outside its sky was always amazing.

The shuttle's engine lit up full force, rocketing the craft across the void. Lintwo placed her files in a pocket on her suit's chest before unlocking her harness and floating over to the cockpit door. Navigating through zero G had been an unnerving experience for many for the first few years.

Lintwo silently watched as the shuttle passed asteroids that had been pulled over for mining. Soon after, the hulking mass of the colony ship took up the shuttle's entire cockpit window. After the shuttle's elaborate dance that was its docking process, Lintwo checked her watch: three hours had passed since takeoff.

Lintwo radioed her pilot and copilot. "You two are getting better at good communication."

The colony ship's crew cranked open the shuttle's hatch. Lintwo floated out as soon as she could. Qilpeea and Cinithea waited for their leader just past where the open space and the pressurized hab units met. After passing through four airlocks, Lintwo met her two friends and began to take off her spacesuit before any of the staff standing by could help her.

"Take me to the farms. We can review the building progress on the way," Lintwo said as she handed the documents she had completed reviewing to Cinithea.

Qilpeea took the lead. The white walls and floors were very clean and sterile-looking. Yellow lighting strips were installed along the floors and walls. No windows dotted the walls in the hallways. Five adults could walk side by side.

The first stop was one of the few places with a pane of glass between the interior of the ship and the void of space. Qilpeea led Lintwo and Cinithea into an elevator. "I hate to admit it, but you have done all right for these people," Qilpeea allowed once they were the only ones in earshot.

Lintwo continued to review documents while taking notes from time to time. "I did what was required of me."

"I know that, so what's your endgame?" Qilpeea asked.

"Use this ship to get close to my target and then take it out," Lintwo replied absently.

"And how long will that take?" Qilpeea pressed.

"At this vessel's theoretical cruising speed, a thousand years or two," Lintwo replied as the elevator dinged and opened to many large garden plots under a stadium-sized glass dome that let some muted starlight in but suppressed most external light, as they were still close to the sun and unprotected by a planet's atmosphere. Lintwo took out a blank piece of paper. "The safety measures in case of a breach?"

"Passed, but for anyone in the dome, it's a death trap," Cinithea reported.

Lintwo noted the response and checked another document before nodding. "As expected then." She handed Cinithea a copy of the document covering the dome's safety.

"You really don't care, do you?" Qilpeea asked.

Lintwo raised an eyebrow. "I do care, but I don't trust anyone approving the finished work. The blueprints and knowledge for the tech area are all mine, after all."

"And you can't share too much because it could be dangerous?" Qilpeea asked.

"That's right, but I'll be around to help keep the ship going," Lintwo said as she walked back to the elevator.

They walked out of the elevator onto one of the decks near the bottom of the ship. A solid third of that deck was an open hydroponics farm.

A twenty-something human man stood near the elevator. His nametag said *Solomon Man*.

Solomon had worked out a way of improving the yield of the farms by just over double. Solomon was one of the children of the people who had followed Samandrea and so was unable to use magic, but was resistant to it.

"Governor," Solomon said, greeting Lintwo by her official title.

"How goes your project?" Lintwo asked.

"The small-scale tests are favorable, but we are still looking at how sustainable it is," Solomon admitted.

Lintwo nodded. "Keep at it," then walked into the deck proper to look over the crops. Some greens but many root vegetables, lentils, and nuts were being grown.

Lintwo had tried to understand farming, but it was not one of her strengths. Killing, leadership, manipulation, organization, and inventing came naturally to her, although most of her inventions were based on knowledge Lindy had given her.

Lintwo looked over the plants; she knew enough to tell if they were healthy. Seeing no visible issues with the foodstuffs, Lintwo turned to Qilpeea. "Next stop, the main reactor."

Qilpeea had shown an affinity for the fission reactor that used the ancient magic generator from Academy 3 as one of its main components.

"This way," Qilpeea said as she resumed leading them.

They exited the farm. A few doors down was the entrance to the silo housing the ship's primary reactor. Three secondary reactors were in the process of being built. Each reactor was housed in a silo that took up space on each deck. The reactor cluster was in the center of the ship.

Qilpeea led the way up a series of gantries, past tubes, wires, transformers, and monitoring panels that could be used to check all the reactors' status.

A low buzz that set bones on edge filled the cylinder, getting more noticeable as they ascended. A kaleidoscopic strobe light effect reflected from the walls. After many floors they reached one of five platforms that encircled a glowing reactor that split magic to generate power by using ice, fire, wind, and earth elemental magic crystals and the main crystal, which was twisted to the point that it mimicked the anti-magic pit Lindy had cursed the world with once.

"Shouldn't this be shielded?" Lintwo asked.

"It's passed all safety tests, but I can divert resources to see that done," Qilpeea said.

"We allocated resources to shield it. Move that up the priority list," Lintwo ordered. The fear of some unknown kind of magic radiation weighed on her mind.

Cinithea led the way up a few more flights and out onto the main command deck, which was far more chaotic than it should be. One of the junior officers ran up to Qilpeea. "Ma'am, we need authorization to go to battle stations."

Lintwo moved in front of Qilpeea. "Explain quickly."

"Our city is under siege," the officer reported stiffly.

Lintwo looked around, finding a team of senior bridge staff talking to Lexi on a comm link. Lintwo rushed over; the message was audio only. Sounds of a heavy firefight echoed across the bridge from the transmission. "They airdropped in," Lexi was explaining.

"How long can you hold?" Lintwo cut in.

Lexi replied, "We are losing ground." An explosion sounded, and a few seconds of static filled the monitor as the command bridge grew quiet, and then Lexi coughed. It was not a good sound. "Not enough time for a shuttle to get back and extract us. I've rigged the city, mines, and oil fields to blow. Take care of yourselves, my family," Lexi said before a shout was heard and the sound shut off.

In the stillness Lintwo raged as others feared. "Get me a visual of the city!" Lintwo shouted.

"We only have the ship's scanners to..." a man began.

"Get eyes on the city. If the best you can do is one pixel, then do it," Lintwo demanded.

The bridge's shot of the world shifted to a high-altitude satellite's perspective, showing a burning city surrounded by sand and an army. Sections of the walls had been cracked open, the oil fields nearby were under attack, and at a few of the towers for the processing centers, firefights were still underway. "By the spirits," an officer cadet muttered.

"We need this recorded," Lintwo muttered, and a few of the staff that were not completely hypnotized by the sight of their 2D home being taken obeyed.

A bright light filled the screen, causing many to look away. A mini supernova had, for the briefest of seconds, marked the world. When the blast ebbed, most of the wasteland was a burning, glass-covered mess where not a speck of dust remained. "We lost another one," Lintwo sighed.

"At least she went out on her own terms," Qilpeea said. She and Lintwo keenly felt the pain of losing another friend.

Lintwo looked around. "We got all that on video?"

A junior officer saluted her. "All recorded, governor."

Lintwo pointed at the screen showing the devastated landscape. "I govern nothing anymore. It looks like I'm just chief architect for now, but I still want that video to be used as part of our standard education."

7

Finding Up

As far as those onboard the ship were concerned, the home world had no place for them, and they had no need of it. Asteroid mining to acquire the materials to finish the ship and reliably harvesting enough food to feed all crew had become priorities.

The people left on the home world had no means yet to escape the planet, as Lintwo had carefully never shared the means of space travel, although a few pieces that led to that had been shared during the war. Sometimes a broadcast message from the home world would be picked up, but those were ignored every time.

Lintwo made sure every new component of the ship met or exceeded her high standards. Above all, the components needed to be reliable and as easy to maintain as possible. Important things like sewage treatment, air, water, and the farms all needed redundancies in case some critical part somewhere failed. If the ship's outer walls were punctured and a passage decompressed explosively, a few safety restraints and emergency masks were provided, but that was mainly for peace of mind, as such things were unlikely to save anyone caught flat-footed. The practical solution was for bulkheads at fixed intervals to seal in the event of a breach. Those trapped within could only pray they had a space suit with a built-in air supply and a good handhold before such an event.

After another year of fevered work that put the productivity of all other years to shame, the ship was completed. A monument with the names of those who had been at their base when the attack started was set on the moon. The service was broadcast to the home world along with a message that read *Play nice, good luck.*

Lintwo watched her home world from the arboretum as the colony ship departed. She had been granted the job of principal of the ship's first college. The position was a tenured one, which meant Lintwo could feasibly hold that office until the ship and college were no more. A small flash of light came from her old home; a city was nuked. "Good luck. You will need it, I guess," Lintwo sighed.

The next few years were slow for Lintwo. Working out lesson plans and hiring the first management personnel for when the current generation of children were old enough to go to college took most of her time in the early years.

After Lintwo turned down the job of captain for the entire colony ship of 1.4 million people, Solomon Man was elected to the job.

Three generations passed before Lintwo saw a potential issue: the officer positions had quickly become staffed by members of the same few now intermarried bloodlines. If not for Lintwo making sure her position was both fully supported by the ship's foundational programming and her position, the ability to sit on the officers' meeting and veto one decision every ten years would have been compromised.

A few from the officers' families had tried to date Lintwo, but she had shot them down each time. Partway through the second generation, Lintwo had taken to wearing a mask when meeting or acting as the principal, as visibly not ageing while appearing as a human or a shade had made her job harder than it needed to be. Generations came and went.

One day an asteroid hit the ship hard when Lintwo was walking back from Cinithea's headstone in the arboretum.

The ship listed, and then the warning lights turned on. Lintwo switched on her radio and called her office. "I'm sorry, but we are in the middle of—" Jenna, her secretary, began.

"JENNA! What's going on?" Lintwo asked firmly.

"Oh, sorry ma'am, sounds like a big rock hit the port side," Jenna Anderson replied.

"Just stay safe. I'll be down soon," Lintwo replied.

"No problem. See you then," the bubbly secretary replied.

Lintwo was able to take the elevator down. She quickly moved through the now slightly off-white hallways, passing by the normal hustle and bustle. However, most crew members moving past her were going in the opposite direction, and security was interspersed in the crowd, helping keep things orderly. From the sound of things, most of the crew believed this was a slightly more elaborate safety drill than normal.

A few security crew broke off from the crowd to help Lintwo push past the lines. The lights flickered a few times in the half-hour trip that was normally five minutes, even with the extra muscle helping Lintwo out.

The doors to the campus were bereft of people as Lintwo slipped inside before letting the security staff get back to their jobs. The campus was dark and unlit save for a side desk near reception where Jenna was typing. Her cubicle was plastered with cartoon frog paraphernalia and a painting of a capybara, a twist sprite, and a honey badger playing cards.

"Jenna!" Lintwo called out.

"What took you so long?" Jenna replied.

"The halls are crammed with people leaving this floor. Thanks for staying. Hand me the notes of what we know so far and get out of here." Lintwo sighed.

Jenna handed her boss three folders of fifty pages each, grabbed her bag, and after a few seconds of looking around, she also scooped up the painting and a frog keychain before rushing out. "Those are in triplicate," Jenna called as she jogged away.

Lintwo looked over the notes, almost forgetting to lock the campus doors on the way out.

Lintwo sprinted through the slowly emptying hallways. The breach had been on two floors of a shopping district. Lintwo met a team of technicians and emergency responders at a door leading to the ship's first big emergency. A few of the younger staff moved to stop Lintwo, but the older ones stopped them.

Lintwo had to take off her mask to fit into a spare space suit, which drew a few surprised glances given how young she still looked. If anyone had a photo from the ship's construction before them, they would have found Lintwo as she looked now there with her ancestors.

Lintwo closed her eyes, sensing the ship's new layout through its shadows and drawing it out before sending the updated map to the lead staff. "There are still a lot of sealed-off rooms in there with limited space and supplies. Do any of you mind if I go in first and test the waters?" Lintwo asked the five highest-ranked people present.

"Is that a good idea, counselor?" one of the more senior members asked.

"You are still planning, right? Don't worry about me," Lintwo said.

The supervisors were troubled. Lintwo was one of a handful of people at the top of the ship's hierarchy. "Just keep in touch. We would never hear the end of it if we lost you." Lintwo smiled sardonically, knowing that the others on the ship's ruling board would be overjoyed to see her vanish, not that many of the rank and file knew that.

Lintwo walked up to the hallway-spanning airlock, the kind that sealed off every section of the ship from every other for times like this. "I'm going scouting," Lintwo told the team leader of the guards at the airlock.

"Alone?" the team leader asked.

"Let her through," one of the senior group leaders radioed over to the gate crew.

Lintwo stepped in and fluidly handled her side of the de-pressurization process and the suit triple-checks. As the last living person who had set those procedures in place at the start, Lintwo would have not settled for anything less. The guard team and technicians handled the process well enough, though with the slowness of those who knew in theory what to do, but cautiously understood that speeding through with the little practical experience they had could end badly.

Finally, Lintwo was released into a rotunda of floating junk and flash-frozen corpses. The chairs and tables at a nearby food court were bolted to the deck with only a dusting of frost. The plants, people, food, and personal effects were ripped apart and frozen, unable to survive the change in pressure, sudden drop in temperature, and lack of atmosphere. The deck still had gravity, but the void did not, and so unsecured things without their own power or a means to resist were being sucked out into space.

The only saving grace was while there had been close to fifteen hundred in the mall, most crew were in school or at work at the time, so the body count could have been far higher.

Lintwo took advantage of her suit's magnetized shoes to slink through the slowly floating debris in search of sealed airtight doors. A young teacher she had interviewed the day before floated by frozen and quite dead, with a smile on the unlucky young woman's face, as she had not even had the chance to realize she was dying. Lintwo watched the skilled teacher she had nearly finished the paperwork to accept as a professor float off towards the jagged gash in the hull where stars glistened without a window to filter them and where only the endless void waited.

Lintwo shook her head. "Tend to the living, then mourn the dead," she reminded herself.

Lintwo checked the first sealed door. It was held open by a delivery cart that had gotten wedged into the doorway, thus keeping it partly open. The next door had not been sealed; instead, it was wide open. The third door was so poorly maintained it had not sealed properly; several bodies were stuck inside. The fourth door was fully sealed and had life signs within. Lintwo tagged the room contents for priority retrieval, making sure her report was clear that there were survivors within.

There was a video call system to contact those within the room. Lintwo called, and not even half a buzz later, a young man answered. "Hello, what's going on?" he asked.

"The mall is exposed to the void, but the rest of the ship is fine. I'm scouting the area. Your location has been relayed to the rescue teams. Sit tight and do not open the door, understood?" Lintwo calmly and clearly explained.

"How long will that take? My wife and daughter are here too," the man said.

"A team will be here as soon as possible. Rest assured you and your family are a priority," Lintwo explained.

"Just be patient. It's enough that they know we are here," a woman's voice said from outside the camera's range.

"I need to check the other compartments nearby," Lintwo continued.

"Ok, thank you," the man said, seeming calmer.

Over the next half hour Lintwo checked many doors, but only four had survivors. The suddenness of the damage had prevented most from knowing to seek shelter, which should not have happened, as the ship's scanners should have picked up something like that rock well before impact. Lintwo knew she would need to investigate.

After checking around, more scouts and rescue teams arrived. Lintwo watched as the rescue teams set inflatable airlocks to the doors with survivors behind them. After much finagling and checking seals, the survivors were led into the portable airlocks and given a once-over before donning space suits and being led back out of the damaged section.

Lintwo moved over to the tear. "Any idea how to fix this, ma'am?" One of the older team leaders radioed her as he moved up to her.

"The fabricators can make a new hull segment given enough time and materials. We may need to find somewhere to mine," Lintwo grumbled.

"That's it?" the man asked.

"What do you know about mining?" Lintwo asked.

"Not much," the team leader admitted. "Is it harder than it sounds?"

"Finding the right materials can be hard, even more so in space," Lintwo admitted, letting her true age show for a second.

Lintwo moved back to the section's exit after she was through with the decontamination protocols and was dressed in normal clothes as well as her mask. Lintwo left only to find the ship's head of accounting in the middle of a tirade demanding a full damage assessment.

"That's enough. Let them work. After maintenance looks over the damage, they can give us an estimate," Lintwo said.

The current head of accounting was a man named Mikiel Sanders. He spun around and glared at Lintwo. "Where have you been?"

"Helping check for survivors." Lintwo shrugged before Mikiel could complain more. Lintwo added, "Let our emergency crews do their work in peace. The last thing we need is mistakes when the ship's safety is at stake."

Lintwo walked away while Mikiel sputtered before getting on a scooter and leaving as well.

The next few days saw Lintwo at her desk going over maintenance logs, casual reports, and the debris forecasts. A few things were not adding up. The maintenance logs did not match the lack of proper maintenance she had seen upon closer examination. The devastated mall was not the only section that showed a lack of repair that had been reported to be fine. The debris forecasts had been clear of any large-scale space junk.

Lintwo had earned a very positive rep as the only top officer who had put herself on the line to help save who she could.

A few days into her investigation, before all her inquiries were answered, a meeting was called.

Qilpee Sagezard, the head of maintenance and the ship's generators, the captain Mandric Man, and the navigator Fronz Man met Lintwo in the bridge's conference room.

Mandric was Fronz's uncle. The Mans were descended from Solomon and had occupied the spots of navigator and captain for a few generations now.

"You have been stepping on the other departments for a while now," Mandric told Lintwo.

Lintwo tossed her current findings over to Qilpee. "Like looking into our lack of repair work?"

Qilpee nodded. "I've looked into that too. We don't have enough raw materials for most repairs unless we actively change course to mine. There has been some embezzlement of maintenance funds that I've been trying to act on."

"Don't worry about it. I've got it under control," Mandric said.

"And the lack of reporting on the rock that killed a few thousand of our crew?" Lintwo pressed.

"Not your concern," Mandric said.

"Is that all?" Lintwo asked impassively while she kept her rage in check.

"No, it's not. You need to stop making trouble for the other departments. It's bad for morale," Fronz said.

"How about you just give her a medal for helping to save so many lives?" Qilpee said.

Mandric glared at the ship's only dragon. "We will see."

Over the next few days Lintwo did her job remotely as she set up a new identity. Jenna helped forward any important calls to a radio Lintwo had made as hard to trace as she could.

Slowly Lintwo integrated her new identity into the ship's least privileged community. She still attended the few events where the college principal had to appear. The council had to suffer Lintwo attending meetings remotely in ways they could not trace. Lintwo dug into reports and other info trying to work out what the most powerful families on board planned because they were stonewalling her. Lintwo concluded they were incompetent or planning some new scheme, and Lintwo preferred to plan and expect the worst while hoping for the best.

Lintwo's new accommodations were on a lower level next to a waste recycling plant, where she found employment on the day shift. During the night shift Lintwo went over the paperwork she needed to fill out and approve for the college.

To gain info, Lintwo began to access the ship's many databanks with a backdoor that had been built in at its conception. This master backdoor was keyed to Lintwo's biometrics for access. She also talked to drunk and dissatisfied folk trying to get a better picture of the council's movements from the ground up.

For Lintwo, time had lost meaning.

One day Lintwo was manning the line that recycled organic matter and a few elements into fertilizer. Corpses, rotting food, and bodily waste, plus some additives, were what made the fertilizer. It was not the hottest or smelliest line, but it did require the most mental fortitude.

Lintwo watched most of a human pass by on the belt. She calibrated the mulcher to account for the extra mass, and once the hopper was full, she punched the button that started the mulcher before looking over at the next wave of refuse coming to her station.

The boss of the fertilizer line came over with one of the new hires and a smartly dressed man. "Reaper, come with me for a sec."

Lintwo looked at the new hire as he walked over to the mulcher with shaky steps. Lintwo followed her direct boss with the out-of-place man as they walked over to an out-of-the-way part of the outer walls. "Reaper, you've killed before, right?" her boss asked.

"Not in a long time." Lintwo shrugged as she watched the stranger.

The smartly dressed stranger sighed, "I can get you a pardon if you help off someone."

"A pardon for what?" Lintwo asked.

"For your past and the job," her boss offered.

If Lintwo was some brat that had grown up in the district and had a hand in some hard crime, like her boss seemed to think after seeing how unfazed she was around death, it would have been a good offer if true. Lintwo smiled thinly. "I'm not just some bilge rat from here. None of my past crimes are known to security," she said truthfully.

Neither of her conversation partners believed her. "Help kill the head of maintenance, Qilpee Sagezard, when she comes next week to review this sector, and all your crimes to this point will be forgiven," the well-dressed man said.

Lintwo knew she had to pretend to agree even if she was going to do everything in her power to save Qilpee and expose those after her. "Fine, but I want a few more sick days too."

Her boss looked like he swallowed a lemon but agreed after his companion nudged him.

The next day Lintwo met a group of five hired killers in a water processing substation. Lintwo had been the first to arrive. Three people arrived half an hour later; the last two trickled in an hour after the meeting-up time.

"You all know what's at stake?" the oldest-looking among them asked.

Someone nudged Lintwo, who had been dozing off and daydreaming about how much extra paperwork she would have to deal with. "My job—any idea who is paying for the hit? I'd like to know so I can avoid them later." Lintwo yawned.

"Why are you so tired?" A tall muscular man snickered.

"Still working full time at the waste processing plant," Lintwo shrugged.

"Will this be a problem?" the old-looking person asked.

"Yes, but I don't have a choice." Lintwo shook her head.

The old man, who was behaving like their self-proclaimed leader, set out a local map with a red line and a few other marks. "Well, the path our target is going along is through here," the self-styled leader said, moving his finger along the red line. "You all have weapons, I'm sure." Lintwo rolled her eyes. "Problem?" the old man asked.

"I don't have any weapons or combat gear. It's been a long time since I've needed something like that," Lintwo replied.

"Then you can be our lookout," the old man said sternly.

Soon after, the meeting broke up. At her home near one of the reactor coolant backups, Lintwo logged into her college principal's account and sent Qilpee a message: *Some people are after you. Watch your back.*

A few seconds later, Qilpee responded, *I know. Some are after you as well.* Lintwo deleted the conversation right after the response and logged off. She spent the next few days planning and working but not really sleeping well except for the day before the hit, when she slept almost all day.

Lintwo met with her temporary team at a bar near Qilpee's publicly given route.

As soon as everyone arrived, their self-proclaimed leader pointed at Lintwo. "Go and keep watch." The others just nodded along, but as Lintwo left, they took out a map and began to work out a rough plan.

Lintwo rolled her eyes and climbed up the side of the bar to sit on its roof and keep watch. Three hours later a group of well-dressed officials moved through the street, keeping the crowds back. The official in the center looked like Qilpee but acted prouder than a dragon, plus they were at least two feet taller. Lintwo slid down the walls of the bar and into it, finding her team mostly drunk. "They will be here in a few minutes," she told the team.

"Then do the job," the youngest of their number demanded while badly slurring his words.

Lintwo gestured to her lack of gear. "With what?"

"How many guards?" the old leader asked.

"Around twenty on the ground, none on the roofs. Most look like pen pushers that had some training, but not professionals," Lintwo replied.

The team began grabbing their stuff. Lintwo went back to the roof and watched.

The hit squad waited until the target and guards were passing right by the bar before unloading explosives and bullets, all of which were outlawed on the ship.

Many of their targets died, but the return laser fire from the guards wounded most of the hit team.

Lintwo jumped down at her team's leader and hit him in the back of the neck, knocking him out. Lintwo took out a knife and rushed at the two assassins that could still move. First she cut the tendons in the legs and arms of one. The other turned to Lintwo and got a palm smashed into his jaw, knocking him out.

The few surviving guards were in no condition to act. The passage was vacated of noncombatants. Lintwo walked over to the target, who was bleeding out on the ground. "You are not the real Qilpee," she noted.

"Help me," Qilpee's body double pleaded.

"I'm not a doctor, and a backup team should be around somewhere." Lintwo sighed. She tore off some of the body double's suit and used the cloth scraps to bandage the wounds as best as she could without jostling the fake too much.

"Why did you help me?" the double asked.

"I needed to capture some of the assassins in hopes they would lead me to the one that hired them," Lintwo replied honestly. "I see you are very cold." The double coughed up some blood. "Just stay awake and don't talk or move," Lintwo requested.

Lintwo hog-tied the still-living assassins before they woke up, then bandaged up the guards that still lived.

A while later a squad of heavily armored paramilitary security members rushed out of a side passage. Lintwo calmly looked up from the wounded she was struggling to tend. "You are late," she said calmly.

A sergeant stepped forward, his laser pistol ready to be raised at a moment's notice. "What happened here?"

"Assassins were able to knock out and tie up some of them. Two are still alive right now," Lintwo replied.

"And who are you?" the sergeant asked.

"Someone that would like to be kept up to date on the investigation," Lintwo said as she stepped back for the team's two medics to check the living and dead.

"We can't do that," the sergeant replied as he twitched.

Someone in the same uniform as the other responders put their hand on the sergeant's shoulder. "Fine, same line as before?" Qilpee asked for anyone that knew her well. The heavy-duty security armor did not hide the dragon at all.

"That works. Can I go? I've got some other folks to hunt down," Lintwo asked.

"Ok, but share what you find," Qilpee demanded.

"That's only fair." Lintwo smiled before rushing off to confront those who had forced the hit on her.

The waste processing facility was fully manned, although a few people wandered around with barely concealed weapons.

Lintwo slipped past the thugs as she tried to hide with the few coworkers late for their shift. Lintwo pretended to punch in before slipping into the facility and into the dimly lit building's shadows as she made her way to the management offices, where the tougher-looking and better-armed thugs roamed.

Lintwo's boss's boss and the self-important man who had been around when she was conscripted for the hit sat around a table.

Lintwo walked up to the guard at the door, who was the only one visibly armed and armored. She froze the man in a block of ice before kicking down the door to the office. "The hit failed," Lintwo smirked.

"Then why are you here, idiot?" her boss's boss asked. Of the three, only her boss was spooked or seemed to notice that Lintwo had easily taken care of the most obvious threat in the building.

"I got a better offer. So who really hired us?" Lintwo smirked.

The other thugs ran up to the office, their weapons brandished. The thugs were smart enough to see their boss's desperation and unwillingness to answer Lintwo, as well as their frozen comrade. They ganged up on Lintwo, all firing at her with low-yield weapons that fired a jolt of electricity unimaginatively called Zap beams.

Lintwo spun and charged at the thugs, carefully avoiding the business ends of the weapons. Lintwo kept low, keeping as many of the thugs as possible in a crossfire of their own making as she lashed out with palm strikes, disorienting her foes and using their firing lines in her favor.

The thugs quickly panicked, but by then Lintwo was in their midst, using one thug after another as cover. In short order the mob of thugs had taken themselves out. As the last fell, Lintwo snatched his weapon and set it to the lowest power setting before firing at the three still-seated targets, stunning them.

Lintwo tied up the thugs, the contact, her foreman, and the foreman's boss with cables before calling Qilpee. "I captured three folks that may know something. Let me sit in on their interrogation, all right?"

"Ok, where do you want to meet?" Qilpee answered on the other end.

"The local recycling center," Lintwo said as she watched the workers flee from the complex.

Lintwo looked through the documents in the office as she waited for her old friend. A while later five very well-armored troops busted into the center, followed by Qilpee and two more lightly equipped people.

Lintwo sat in the center of the office while one of the troopers who checked the office fired at her, but Lintwo tilted her head, dodging. Qilpee rushed over. "She's with us," the dragon explained.

Lintwo slowly pointed at a few hefty piles of possibly in-criminating documents—everything from odd correspon-dences to expense sheets that did not add up. "That's all the odd paperwork I've found so far. I'll stay and watch the inter-rogation here as agreed."

Before any of her support could complain, Qilpee nodded and sat down. "That's only fair after all your help."

Qilpee let her two less well-armed aides place their hands on the captives' heads and close their eyes. The prisoners be-gan to scream. Lintwo raised an eyebrow. Quilpee said, "Never seen a telepath before? It's a form of psionics that's not the same as magic. These two are some of the first to de-velop such abilities."

"I've heard of it, but those powers are rare. You know the overall strength and magic powers of the crew are also on the rise," Lintwo said defensively.

"Well, the homeworld had a lot that weakened magic," Qilpee noted as she watched Lintwo with one eye.

"True," Lintwo easily agreed.

One of the aides walked over to his boss. "The Man family paid to have you killed, boss."

Qilpee looked at Lintwo; they both just rolled their eyes in understanding that this news was unsurprising. Qilpee was slightly jealous that her old friend had managed to escape having to regularly deal with the council's nagging and power plays.

Qilpee walked out of the room. Her guards and aides quickly followed. "We will be in touch," Qilpee promised.

"Sure," Lintwo waved as she pondered what to do with the still tied-up prisoners. After some pondering, Lintwo sighed and asked herself what Lindy would do.

Two hours later the Man family's cleanup crew arrived due to an anonymous tip placed in their secure servers. They found three disposable pawns attached to the side of a waste reprocessing plant with a lot of glue and wrappings made of documents incriminating the Man family and its agents.

Lintwo watched from the growing and very inquisitive crowd. She almost felt physical pain thinking of the chaos to come, but revealing herself or lugging the pawns through the ship was not an option, so this was the next best thing she could work out on short notice.

Lintwo walked back to her unimportant civilian identity's home. The messaging system of her principal identity was already overflowing with messages marked urgent. She ignored them for the day, going to bed early after a stiff drink.

The next morning Lintwo did not go to work. Instead, she sat down and began the long process of looking through her messages.

8

Some Things...

Days passed. Lintwo's life changed little. She kept attending meetings virtually; sometimes she made appearances at the college. Each time a new member of the council was elected, Lintwo would show up in person. Two more generations passed. Friends and acquaintances died, and new ones were found.

Lintwo's less wealthy persona moved from job to job every ten years or so in different sectors of the ship where the less well-off had begun to congregate.

Those in the Man family who had planned to attain Qilpee's job were disowned. All blame was set on that part of the family. Neither Lintwo nor Qilpee fully believed that claim but chose not to say as much in public, as hopefully this debacle was enough of a warning.

Lintwo's current apartment was in one of the ship's many growing shanty towns, set in an old storage hold that had failed far too many safety inspections. She worked in a maintenance team that was given some of the messier and/or dangerous tasks. Sadly, it was not easy to harvest new supplies, let alone make new parts that were as good as the ship's original parts.

Lintwo had just returned from a grueling 18-hour shift where three of her coworkers died. She sat on her porch in time to see a streak of blond and a hint of a very clean college uniform running through the shanty town. A few well-known hooligans passed by soon after. Lintwo grumbled as she rushed out after them.

The hooligans' prey was fast but far from stealthy or just too panicked to mind. Lintwo stalked through the slums even more unimpeded than normal, as the roads had been temporarily cleared by those who still pretended to not see anything, not thinking just how much of a shitstorm a disappeared or dead student could be for their little slice of life.

Lintwo went unnoticed by the few who peered at this rare flavor of ongoing drama. Masking her steps and presence had long become second nature. In a tight alleyway that had once been a side street, if not for the five dumpsters crammed into it, the hooligans had cornered their prey.

Lintwo rounded the corner and grabbed the arm of the biggest hooligan, who was going to grab what Lintwo realized was a young woman in the sociology major. Lintwo broke and twisted the man's arm. "Hey, this is not your gang's turf."

Over the man's screams, Lintwo looked up at the hooligans and said with an icy calmness, "Going after an easy mark I understand, but when it's some well-to-do outsider from the college on another crew's turf, do you chumps have a death wish?"

"Look, Mist, the Beavers let us pass," one of the hooligans sputtered.

Lintwo rolled her eyes and let the big hooligan go. "Don't care. You Frogs used to be smarter. Now run. I'll drag this idiot out so security does not burn our home to the ground."

The hooligans from the Frogs dragged their big comrade away. No one in the slums called Lintwo by her name anymore; they simply called her Mist, a nickname for how stealthy she could be, given more from fear than respect. To be fair, most had likely forgotten her name, and Lintwo did not try to remind them.

"I'm not an easy mark," the student said as she picked herself up from the grime-covered ground.

Lintwo looked at the student with impassive eyes. "Says you. Come on, I'm bringing you out of here."

"Not without answers," the student said, holding her ground.

Lintwo held out her hand. "Fine, I'll give you the scenic route and answer what I want to, but you are not coming back here."

The student shook her hand. "Tara Maxillius, sociology major."

Lintwo tightened her grip and began to lead Tara away. "Mist, one-time tour guide."

Lintwo led Tara through the Frogs' territory without issue. The streets remained empty as the locals hid.

"Why is no one here?" Tara asked.

Lintwo stopped at a red-painted laundromat, which marked the border of the Frog and Beaver territories on this street. "It's not empty now, is it, gentlemen?" Lintwo called out.

All thirty of the remaining Frogs and twenty of the Beavers stepped out from the sides of the streets. "No, it's not. Hand over the brat, Mist," Gen, the leader of the Frogs, said.

Lintwo let go of Taras's hand and pulled out a hunk of pipe with large bolts attached. "Not on your life."

"Then you die," Gen said as his men raised their weapons and charged. Almost none of them had ranged weapons, as such things were heavily restricted. Blades and clubs were the tools of the day.

Flames formed around Tara's hands as she activated her pyrokinesis. Lintwo looked around, not liking her chances of defending Tara while not using her full shade-like powers.

Lintwo's shadow extended and enveloped Tara.

Tara was transported from the slums to a girl's student restroom at the college.

Gen narrowed his eyes at Lintwo, but before he could fully analyze what had happened, a shadow-covered dagger flew from his shadow into the back of his head. The rest of the gang members sank into their own shadows while the dagger shot from one shadow, through one or two people, and into the next. After a few seconds of this repeating, the street was quiet. The shape-changing knife known as The End sank back into Lintwo.

The bodies and blood were absorbed by the dankness of the street before being chucked out into space as the ship continued cruising on its long journey.

In the college restroom, Tara opened her eyes. She looked at her hands, not remembering when they had begun shaking or when she had closed her eyes. Tara sat in the restroom for a long while, coming to terms with the fact that Mist was likely dead by now.

Tara staggered through the college to her dorm room. Tara's roommate Sandmera was sitting at a desk going over a long-term group project. "You are back early. Didn't make it to the workers' quarter?"

"I don't want to talk about it," Tara grumbled as she made her way to her bed.

Sandmera turned around. "Well, tomorrow can you help with our group project?"

Tara watched the clean white metal ceiling, comparing it to the dingy and poorly maintained slums. "Our project was about why the ship was created?" she asked.

Sandmera walked over and held an old image in front of her friend's face. The image was of the wake held for the ship's ground team that did not flee the home world in time.

Tara looked over the faces before setting her eyes on the main podium in the image, where someone stood who looked exactly like Mist. Tara sat up and grabbed the image. "I need to go back."

"Back? Why?" Sandmera asked.

"I met someone that looks exactly like the speaker in this image," Tara explained.

Sandmera thought for a few seconds. "Ok, we will get a few of our friends and go down tomorrow. No more running off on your own."

"Wait until tomorrow?" Tara asked.

"Yes, tomorrow you will still look terrible. Get some sleep," Sandmera insisted.

The chime for the work cycle resetting rang through the ship, signaling the start of a new day. Tara jumped out of bed. In her heart of hearts she knew a normal person would have had very little chance of winning against the numbers Mist had faced for her, but Mist seemed anything but normal, so Tara chose to believe that Mist was able to escape.

Sandmera was already dressed and washed up when Tara looked over at her friend's side of the room. Sandmera handed Tara a cup of coffee. "Are you sure you still want to look for your new acquaintance?"

Tara sipped the coffee. "Yes. I don't feel right leaving her behind."

Sandmera rubbed her eyes. "I asked Catrin from the security course and Josh from the engineering course to come with us, and they agreed. A few others agreed before the news a few hours ago." She handed Tara a handheld computer. A secret alert was penned on it stating that a riot had broken out on the worker decks and to expect cleaning crews to be delayed. No other riots in the past had that second part tacked on.

Tara stared at the computer. "What's going on down there?"

"Nothing good. So are you still going?" Sandmera asked with concern.

Tara's hands shook, and she bit her lip before croaking, "Yes, I am."

Sandmera handed Tara one of two bags. "This was all I could find that may help. Get dressed, and let's go down there before this gets worse."

Tara grabbed the bag and rushed to the bathroom to clean up and get dressed. Sandmera called after her friend, "If I ask you to run, we run, ok?"

"Right," Tara nodded, knowing that this would not be a cakewalk.

Tara and Sandmera met Catrin and Josh at an oddly empty lift. Tara hit the button for one of the lower floors, but the lift remained open. Josh took out his phone and searched for some info on a secure engineering chat site. "The lower levels are locked down."

Catrin punched in a borrowed code to override the lift; only then did it descend.

The floors became less and less eternal white and more gray as the lift rocked in the arbitrary direction of down.

The lift lurched as it arrived at their destination. The four exited cautiously. The floor was empty and quiet in all but their chosen destination.

The friends crept forward to find a mass of huddled people cowering behind a large security detachment that stood by the airlock to the main workers' hab block. A shadow expanded by the huddled people. One of the security crew glanced back and huffed, "Another one." Shortly after a person landed in a lump by the other huddled and scared civilians.

"Whoever is sending out dead weight from this gang war needs to stop. It's annoying," another guard sneered.

"The head engineer is too nice. They should be working," another guard complained.

Head engineer Qilpee walked over from the front of the airlock. Tara and friends hid in a side passage and began looking for another way in. As they escaped, Qilpee's voice boomed, "Oh, are you three volunteering to go in and stop this mess right now?"

"No, ma'am," the three vocal guards replied stiffly.

"Then shut up," Qilpee ordered.

Josh led his friends down a side passage until they arrived at a vent that looked just like hundreds of others they had passed. "This should be it." Josh nodded as he opened a toolbox and began prying open the vent.

"Destroying an access point is highly illegal," Catrin noted.

"Destroying a door, shutter, or other access point's ability to lock down, preventing depressurization, is illegal. These shutters have a separate airtight shutter that only comes down when a hull breach is detected nearby," Josh replied, not bothering to look up from his work.

"Someone's prepared," Catrin joked.

Soon the shutter was open. "One of us has to know the laws," Josh smirked.

"Show off." Catrin shook her head before crawling into the vent first.

Tara, Sandmera, and lastly Josh crawled after their friend. It was a tight and winding path. The sound of gunfire reached their ears as it echoed within the vent. At the end of the shaft, Catrin kicked open the shutter and jumped down. Her friends followed.

Sandmera wanted to use her water magic to clean them of the dirt her friends had picked up in the vents, but the firefight all around them was a more pressing matter.

"How did they get all that firepower?" Josh asked before noting that Catrin had drawn her own sonic projector.

From around some debris, a man with a hunk of pipe rushed them. Catrin raised her weapon and shot concentrated sound at him. Most people would be incapacitated and feel very ill from such an attack, but the man only staggered before charging with even more gusto. Catrin panicked and raised her weapon's output. The man staggered one more time before his head exploded.

The group had no time to process the first violent death any of them had seen before someone with a knife rushed at them from another direction. Catrin moved swiftly, but a stray bullet fired from someone else hit their new attacker, grazing the knife wielder's neck. The knife wielder took two faltering steps as blood rushed from his carotid artery, then collapsed.

The group was lucky this time but did not feel lucky at all. Tara looked around. "We can't stay in this spot," she said.

Josh looked at Catrin, who was still shaken from killing someone, and pointed. "There's a maintenance office that way. Those are very secure and built like bunkers. Catrin and I know the codes."

Sandmera said, "Lead the way, but don't rush," as she grabbed Catrin's hands.

The group managed to slip past a few more firefights by staying low and putting big chunks of debris between themselves and most of the mobs.

Across the street from the maintenance office, the team saw the door was open with a small child hiding beside it. A firefight closed in on the maintenance office as two groups leapfrogged from cover to cover, escaping the bulk of the fighting.

Tara wanted to rush to the child, but her friends held her back. Before the firefight reached the office, an inky puddle formed at the child's feet, and with that, the child was gone.

One of the two approaching armed groups rushed around to use Tara and company's cover. Both groups froze, but a black knife came out of nowhere and slit the first group of thugs' necks. Soon after, Sandmera's shadow extended, revealing Mist sitting down, bloody and out of breath. Tara held out her arm, stopping her friend from attacking.

"I told you not to come back," Mist panted.

Josh and Catrin peeked out from behind cover to find the other group of nearby attackers dead in the street, their bodies torn open.

Sandmera looked over her friend's acquaintance. On closer inspection, Mist looked 100% like one of the ship's founders, minus the dirt and blood. "Can you evacuate us the same way as the other refugees?" Sandmera asked, taking a shot in the dark, but sure enough, she was right.

"Not until my energy recharges. I'm running dry as it is." Mist shook her head and pulled out a pistol.

Catrin watched as Mist peeked over their cover. "But you cast just now, right?"

"I've been using my blood as a substitute for any more casting, and I'll pass out," Mist explained. This was not a technique the four friends knew about. The study of how to use magic had only begun again in the last generation, after all.

"I've never heard of that," Tara admitted.

Mist fired five shots into the distance. The bullets she was using were designed to damage only soft targets. Anything hard would shatter the bullets, mostly harmlessly. Four thugs yelled, "We need to move now!" "Talk later," Mist told them. To the four friends the firefight sounded much the same, but Lintwo "Mist" Reaper could tell it was slowly getting closer to them.

"We should hide in the maintenance office," Catrin noted.

"That's a prime target for looters, and it has one way in," Mist explained.

"Then what's your suggestion?" Catrin demanded.

Mist pointed in the direction of the maintenance office. "There's a small abandoned warehouse that way. In a few hours I can send you four out."

"We should hurry," Tara said.

"Follow me, but keep low." Mist nodded as she began to slowly skirt around the rubble. The four followed. Mist led them quickly across a narrow street and around a few buildings before arriving at a rundown but intact blocky building with three thick steel doors.

They slowly entered the building and looked around. It was empty of life but not of junk. They used the intact furniture to barricade the doors. Mist and company took up positions on the second floor, peeking out of windows.

After a few more hours the firefights spread out as the fighters tried to disengage and rest up, but to Tara's dismay, the ship's security remained holed up outside.

At some point the fans began to activate as the air was jettisoned into space. Mist grabbed her four acquaintances and evacuated them to the other refuges. Qilpee was angrily on a radio when they returned, but a few security guards flinched when Mist and company arrived.

Josh looked at his handheld. "They aren't sending the air to the scrubbers; it's being jettisoned."

"There should be a big enough reserve to fill that room back up," Mist said as her eyes closed and she passed out from exhaustion.

A few hours later Lintwo opened her eyes. A tent was over her head, but the floor was still the same. Qilpee sat in a folding chair nearby; the dragon's hair had a few gray spots now. "So Mist, I hear we have you to thank for getting some of the crew out alive."

"The board tell you they were spacing the atmosphere?" Lintwo demanded.

"No, they did not. The college president was left out as well, I'd imagine," Qilpee replied. Both had appearances to keep up. The thin wall of cloth around them did nothing to hide their voices from those outside.

"So is the workers' quarter safe to go back into yet?" Lintwo asked.

"It is being cleaned out of bodies and debris right now. The orders for a Misty Reaper are to help man the smelters, which are being run as a crematorium," Qilpee said.

"Of course that's the plan," Lintwo sighed. She was disappointed things had come to this.

"If you don't like it, then get to a place where your voice can be heard," Qilpee said. Her tone was scathing, but for reasons only they knew.

Lintwo sat up and walked out of the tent. Her double life had finally come back to bite her hard. "No more running away," she sighed.

Outside the tent and past security teams, the refugees who had been sitting around were gone. She walked past grumbling squads of armed government-sponsored toughs, who were just cleaner and worse-armed than the better-armored thugs. The massive airlock into the workers quarter was unlocked, but the guards were making a show of making entry and exit hard by slowly following all the regulations, many of which she knew had not been used in hundreds of years on any big scale. The scans of every cavity were not supposed to be done on a large scale, only on suspicious people and/or on a random basis, which the teams seemed to read as all the workers.

Lintwo knew the extra checks would slow down the day's cleaning, which would just make everyone even more agitated. Some guards worked out of fear, others out of hate, and others out of obedience to the system.

Lintwo worked hard to resist simply teleporting past the checks, but she did make sure her weapons and other combat gear were tucked inside her shadow. Lintwo let her mind wander as she was checked over, poked, prodded, and scanned for a good twenty-five minutes before being shoved into the airlock and let back into the workers' quarter with a temporary pass clenched in her hand.

As she walked to her posting, Lintwo passed mounds of bodies being piled up by friends, family, and neighbors. Makeshift sleds made of scrap were being pulled by groups of people through the junk-filled streets. Here and there, looters ran around. All this while security looked on, disgusted by their fellow humans but not stepping in or taking their hands off their weapons.

Lintwo had to slip through a few alleys to avoid the mass of raging humanity all around her. At some point she arrived at the smelters. A few coworkers from the maintenance team were present, but only a handful acknowledged her, their eyes and minds showing their distress, sorrow, and exhaustion.

Lintwo sighed at the signs that another riot would follow unless the leaders of their ship acted like they cared, knowing that one of those that could and should step up was her other identity.

After a while of chucking bodies into a smelter, someone nearby said "Hey boss! Boss!" before tapping Lintwo on the shoulder.

Lintwo transitioned over to check the fuel and heat levels of her station. She glanced behind her. "I'm not management," Lintwo said to one of her team's new hires.

"Well, you are the most senior member left in our department," the crewman said. A few crew members flinched at the mention of their missing or dead colleagues.

"I'm sorry, what?" Lintwo demanded.

"You are the boss of the maintenance department on this level now. That's what the sign-in system said," the crew member said.

Lintwo groaned before clearing her throat and bellowing, her voice carrying over the chaos like it had back on the home world. "Listen up, business as normal. We will have plenty of overtime for the next few days, so look alive. This is our home, so we will clean it up! Anyone that does not gripe too loudly will get bonus pay."

"We never even get overtime," a crewmember with close to Lintwo's service record mumbled loudly.

"And I'll kick anyone that refuses to pay up! Now back to work," Lintwo replied, her voice reverberating above the sizzling of bodies and the smelter's infernal hum.

9

Stay the Same

The council convened. Qilpee got to the boardroom early despite the captain and navigator being on the main bridge one door away. This generation's security chief was late as always. Once all four were assembled, they moved to begin, only for the door to open and a member walked in who none of the other three had seen in person since getting their jobs. Then the chief of academics walked in. Her uniform was a little looser than it had been. Before anyone could ask what was going on, all cameras in the room shut down and the doors locked.

The captain, Samuel Man, moved to pull out his gun, thinking they were under attack. His son, Ronuss Man, the navigator, almost followed suit. Kenith Davenross was slow on the draw as usual, his hangover more pressing than the presumed threat among them.

The chief of academics slowly took off her mask and slammed it on the desk. Everyone remembered her face. Each time someone became a high officer and joined the council, the head of the college and chief of academics showed them her face just once. Of the current officers, only Qilpee had seen her old friend's face more than once and knew where to find her.

"I'll be attending in person more often from now on," Lintwo announced as she literally stared down the barrel of the captain's gun.

"Why are you here?" Samuel asked, unnerved that the one he knew only as The Principal did not look even a minute older than she had fifty years before when they had last met face to face.

The terminals in front of each officer pinged as the agenda was updated. *Approving workers' overtime pay* was now top of the agenda. "It's at the top of the list because I expect this will take a while." Lintwo smiled.

"You can't just change the agenda like that," Ronuss sputtered.

"The good principal has always had the ability to command the ship's systems. We may as well get this over with and hope she goes through the proper channels later," Kenith said, sounding far more sober than he felt.

Guns were slowly put away. "Ok, why should we pay more?" Samuel asked.

"Because the workers need to feel they are part of the crew. We can't have a second airless massacre," Lintwo said.

"Is that what they are calling our suppression operation?" Kenith garbled.

"Yes, it's an apt moniker," Qilpee replied.

"The workers are part of the crew you used the stick on; now we need the carrot," Lintwo explained slowly. Her proposal was swiftly approved. Lintwo put on her mask again and napped through the rest of the meeting, as all her overtime hours had taken a toll.

Lintwo got home late after nearly three hours of sneaking back, while losing those her fellow council members had sent to tail her. The next morning she almost woke up late.

When Lintwo got to her team's maintenance office, she found most of her staff looking over an announcement bolted to the front door. "Hey boss, looks like you are moving up in the world," one of them said.

Lintwo pushed open the door. "Sure, whatever," she grumbled, still half asleep.

"Try to look a little happy. You are getting transferred to the college as a student, all expenses paid," another of her coworkers said.

Lintwo spun around. "WHAT!" she shouted. Rushing back to the door, Lintwo ripped off the metal plaque bolted to the door and read over it. In far more flowery and long-winded language, the notice said just what her coworkers had summarized, although they had left out that she was being replaced as the new boss of her team by a rotating team of students the ship's officers would choose.

At the college later that day, just after lunch, Tara was walking to a class only to find someone in a dust-covered jumpsuit lugging three duffel bags down the halls. "Mist?" Tara asked.

Lintwo looked up. "Oh hey, Tara, see you in class later."

Tara watched the one she knew as Mist strut down the hall like she owned the college, leaving a trail of dirt. "Sandmera is going to go nuts when I tell her about this," Tara smirked.

Sandmera knew about Mist being admitted to the college before Tara told her.

Both Tara and her roommate almost got to class late because Sandmera would not stop talking about Mist. Mist was in their first class as well, but she looked far more tired than they did, like it was taking all her willpower not to fall asleep with her eyes open.

Maolo Fisk was the first-period teacher. When he entered the room, the students quieted down and quickly cleaned up the tops of their desks.

Mr. Fisk did a quick head count before announcing, "Don't open your textbooks. Just open the app for this class and try to solve as many of the problems as you can."

Lintwo took out a slightly battered tablet and opened the app for her math class. All the textbooks and class info could be loaded onto a tablet. Some teachers used the tech more than others.

Mr. Fisk watched the class and answered questions as needed. Lintwo made sure some of her worded answers were less complex than what was needed, as it would be odd for her current identity to be at a college level on her "first" day.

In the next classes, history, economics, shop, gym, and physics, the teachers took a similarly standoffish approach, although shop took place in a warehouse filled with machining equipment and gym took place in the sports field. Somehow Lintwo was near the head of the class in the academic subjects and was top of the class in shop and gym despite trying to not take the courses too seriously, instead observing the other students and teachers.

Lintwo's pride made her still try for a good grade even if she was not trying for the best, and many generations of double-checking the professors' grading gave her an unfair advantage with some of the more nuanced problems. By the end of her first day, Lintwo had a bigger target on her back than at the start.

Lintwo walked to her dorm room. Tara, Sandmera, and Catrin walked in the same direction a few steps back. So far no one had verbally accosted Lintwo.

Lintwo arrived at a room labeled unit 184c ½. She was sure of two things: last time she checked, no dorm rooms had a number ending with a fraction, and her assigned room had been a broom closet until very recently.

When Lintwo unlocked her door, Catrin walked over, asking, "What are you doing?"

Lintwo chuckled as she saw the small cot and battered footlocker in the otherwise empty and very tiny room. "Opening my door." Lintwo's mind swirled with thoughts of how to make the lives of the staff members behind her room assignment difficult.

Tara peeked into the former broom closet next to her dorm room. "That's not a room."

"It is now. Good night," Lintwo replied before entering her room and shutting the door.

The next day an announcement was posted on Lintwo's door that she was to report to the maintenance office in the workers' quarter to be the leader of the cleaning crews for the day as part of a new work-study initiative. This new order renewed Lintwo's resolve to find out who was behind her current identity's treatment.

Catrin exited her room, which was across from Tara and Sandmera's. Catrin walked over to Lintwo. "Hey, Mist, are you ready for class?"

Lintwo stepped aside, letting Catrin read the work notice. After some very expressive shifts in her face, Catrin said, "But you just got here."

Lintwo nodded. "And I'm going to be late. See you later." Catrin watched her new friend run off, feeling both concerned and angry for her friend's sake.

Lintwo quickly walked to a set of elevators off the main thoroughfare. She stood aside for a cleaning crew that was trying to shove a cart out of the elevators. When the cleaning crew got out of the elevator, the oldest member held the door open for Lintwo and simply bowed their head. "Thanks. Keep up the good work," Lintwo said as she got into the elevator, knowing that even petty kindness was rare.

Lintwo leaned against the elevator wall as it rocketed down to the bowels of the ship, her eyes closed. "How did I let things get this bad?" Lintwo sighed. She knew that the bulk of the crew would have to change their mindset before people were kinder to their fellow humans. The only thing she could have done was not hide as much, but that would have complicated things.

Lintwo soon arrived at her floor and quickly got out of the way of another cleaning crew. Lintwo bobbed and wove through crowds as all adults on the ship learned to do, although only a handful still recalled when that was not as important to their ancestors.

The airlock to the slums was ajar, allowing unfettered access. The main streets were nearly clear, although a few side paths were more cluttered than a few days before. Lintwo arrived unhindered at her workplace. Her coworkers she remembered, and a bunch of new faces looked up. "Hey, Mist, heard you were our first overseer."

Lintwo shrugged. "So I'm told. What priority requests are there for us?"

A greenhorn she did not recognize spoke up. "They are all priority."

"I am not asking what the requests are labeled as. What tasks will affect the health and safety of the ship most?" Lintwo replied coolly.

A coworker who had joined a few months before her spoke up. "A few of the old coolant pipes around here are filled with junk and bodies."

"Right, that's our kind of job. Suit up and give me a list of requests that need doing around those pipes. You all have five minutes starting now," Lintwo said before walking over to her old locker and grabbing her pressurized and armored hazmat suit.

The team walked through the crowded streets. Normally the team leader would be in the middle, but Lintwo led from the front. She reviewed other requests, only approving those most of the locals would have trouble with. Some collapsed tenements, a gas leak in a ruined ventilation system, and an old warehouse turned school with half the building starting to sag were all accepted.

When they arrived at the pipes, Lintwo split the team. Most of the more experienced members went with Lintwo to the coolant pipe. Six of the older members with leadership experience went with the younger members to the other jobs.

The path through the coolant pipes was damp with old runoff pooling from who knew how many places, filling a few inches on the path. Half a mile in, the heaps of junk began: old parts, trolleys, and more undefinable scrap. Lintwo left most of her team with the scrap and went further in soon after they began to find the bodies. Most of the corpses were relatively new, likely dumped or washed away from the riots. A handful were very old, maybe by a few years, but no lab would care enough to double-check.

After double-checking some maps, Lintwo worked out that the bodies were almost all located near a junk-clogged sluice gate connected to a mining ship dock near the outer hull.

The first order of business was making sure the sluice gate remained sealed. Most of the maintenance systems on it were inoperable, but the few left were linked to other nearby pipes, so a bypass for the coolant would be sent to other pipes in the network.

Lintwo made it her job to look over the older bodies. All the bodies were damaged from debris and water, so finding a conclusive cause of death was next to impossible, even more so with no gear. Two bodies, however, were wearing environmental suits, one an older version of her team's and the other a cutting-edge space suit not even a few months old. The newer suit had no ID associated with it. The older one had belonged to the first navigation team back when the colony ship was being built but had not been assigned to another group, as far as Lintwo could access remotely from the network as Mist.

"How long overdue are his payments?" one of her team asked, looking at the old suit. The near sarcasm was valid given her team technically rented antiques and was charged extra for the use of 'cultural artifacts' despite said artifacts being far less effective than the newest suits.

"This one's last recorded use was when the ship was still being built," Lintwo replied as she looked over the old suit's destroyed air filters.

The day moved slowly. Even after the manual labor was done, Lintwo had to stay behind to fill out many reports. It was well into the night shift when she returned to the college, but even then, she had work to do.

Lintwo snuck into her room and grabbed a case with the outfit she wore as the principal. She changed in one of the restrooms before going to the principal's office.

Lintwo spent the rest of the night looking into information only a member of the council had access to and brainstorming how to stay a step ahead.

Two hours before the day shift began, Lintwo noticed a security update saying that a student named Tara was demanding to see the principal.

Lintwo hit her buzzer to her receptionist. A lot of yelling echoed through the audio feed. "Let her in," Lintwo ordered.

Tara rushed into the principal's office only to find a huge pile of paperwork with someone much shorter than she expected wearing the current generation's principal's mask. "I thought you would be taller," Tara said before cursing herself and taking a deep breath to try to calm down.

"Close the door," the principal commanded without sparing her a glance. Tara froze. "And stay on my side of the door. I'll hear out your complaint in person this once," the principal added.

Tara quickly shut the door. "This may take a while," she began.

"This is about the transfer student you have been following? I am well aware of you two. Only tell me your complaint, and I will tell you if I need more details. But assume I know the background," the principal said, still filling out paperwork when digital systems were so much more efficient.

"Mist is not being given the full education promised. Her new tasks have nothing to do with schooling, and now she is missing," Tara explained, the words spilling out as she fought to keep them concise. For better or worse, the principal was her last hope; no other leadership or faculty cared to hear her out to this point, although many were simply beyond her ability to talk to.

The sound of the principal's pen stopped, and the full weight of her regard crashed into Tara. "Is that all?" The principal enunciated slowly; the deliberate force of her words almost crushed Taras's heart and hope. "Your friend is fine; she will return soon. You may leave."

Tara willed herself to stand firm and not move an inch despite sweating and trembling. Something about the principal was both powerful and wrong, more so than anyone else, but Tara had never heard anyone describe their often-absent principal like that. "No, tell me where she is. I need to help her." Tara hoped her newest show of civil disobedience was not her last.

The principal crossed her arms and looked up at the ceiling. Seconds felt like months before the principal quickly growled and removed the mask. "Fine, but you will help me get back at the council for their interference," Mist her friend said from the principal's chair in the principal's clothes...

In the principal's office... "WAIT, WHAT?" Tara demanded.

Mist rolled her eyes and began tossing the principal's mask up and down. The former suffocating pressure was gone. "First, I am the principal and always have been; please don't tell anyone. Anyway, how would you like to be my assistant along with our shared friend Mist? How would you like that, my good friend and classmate?"

"So you aren't Mist, and this is some sick joke?" Tara asked carefully.

"Oh, I am Mist, but I have been called many other names as well," Mist replied. In her shock Tara could only nod. None of this seemed real, but her friend continued after a short pause. "Ok, well, the two of us will come here after class today. I believe the captain's grandson is taking over my shift in the so-called workers' sector today."

"That's it?" Tara asked, still not sure what was up or down.

"That's right, see you soon. Just act normal and don't share anything I told you," Mist said as she donned the principal's mask.

Tara left on shaky legs but caught her friend grumbling, "I swear that's the last time I act like Mom. No way that mindset is healthy."

Lintwo spent the rest of the day doing paperwork as the principal. Her plan to use the ongoing power plays to keep her alter ego down affected others, while pretending to be blissfully ignorant was time-consuming.

The first to call her was the ship's captain. "Why is my grandson being assigned to an overseer detail?" he demanded, skipping the pleasantries. He even had the gall to override Lintwo's ability to decline the call.

"The new transfer you assigned to my care was placed back at her old job while still being assigned to classes here as part of a work-study program. I am very glad my staff took the initiative to enact such an inspired program, but it is woefully lacking in candidates so I've resolved that issue," Lintwo replied with faked joy.

"But why my grandson?" the captain pressed.

"I'm only going down the list of this week's top-scoring students. As your grandson is second, it seemed only logical," Lintwo replied, this time with real joy.

The captain's grandson was constantly at the top of all his classes, although Lintwo suspected some of that was due to the teachers helping him. "Then send the new top scorer first," the captain demanded.

"We already did. Misty Reaper was sent to her old job yesterday," Lintwo replied, taking great care to hold back her glee.

The captain looked through some documents before snapping, "Impossible, my grandson was bested by the new transfer."

"That's right. Miss Reaper set a record for the highest scores on record," Lintwo said.

"You did this," the captain accused her.

"I am only enacting your inspired intuition to be more inclusive," Lintwo said happily.

The captain took a few seconds to compose himself. "I'm just surprised by your speed. Good day." The communication was then cut with haste.

Lintwo took a few seconds to look round her room, waiting for another call. When none came, she burst out in laughter, decades of stress melting away in a single moment.

"I really should not play around with this, but damn, it's been so long since I've messed up their plans so much with so little. No, I can't become like Mom. I need to take this more seriously." Lintwo gasped as she got her mirth under control.

After Lintwo spent a few more hours sorting out her growing pile of paperwork that read more like complaints, Tara arrived at her office again. Before another argument could break out in reception, Lintwo opened the door and called out, "Come in, my new assistant." The door shut when Tara rushed in.

"Can you do something about those glares?" Tara asked.

"Reception and security giving you a hard time?" Lintwo asked.

"What did you expect? Even the instructors are giving me weird looks," Tara snapped, knowing it was her friend under the principal's mask.

"Right, well, that's going to go on for a while now. Help me finish up these complaint forms," Lintwo said as she split her paperwork in half and pulled a chair out of her shadow.

Tara spent the next few hours helping her friend ignore and file away most of the current paperwork, of which complaints and thinly veiled threats were the majority. All the while Tara debated what to tell Sandmera.

That night Lintwo and Tara got back to the dorm near midnight. On Tara's door was a note from Sandmera. It read, *I've got to help examine a new discovery. Don't wait up.*

The next day Sandmera was still not back. Lintwo and Tara went to class, in which they both half listened and half slept.

That night after some more paperwork, principal Lintwo, as Mist, arrived back at her dorm room to find Tara and Catrin confronting Sandmera.

"I can't tell you about where I was." Sandmera said, her tone firmer than normal.

"You couldn't even tell us you were going to be away?" Tara asked.

"It's classified," Sandmera said with a grimace.

"No, it's not," Lintwo replied.

"Wait, you know?" Catrin asked.

"Some artifacts were found that led to old records from a mining craft whose crew dispersed fifty years ago," Lintwo said.

"And the ship was located on board," Sandmera grumbled, "but nothing more than that."

"It's classified for now, I know." Lintwo nodded.

"But how did you know that?" Catrin demanded.

"My team found one of these artifacts. The principal had me look into some of the documents." Lintwo nodded.

"The principal?" Sandmera asked.

"Right, get this: Tara and the new kid are aides to the principal now," Catrin bragged on her friend's behalf.

"Just like that?" Sandmera asked.

"That's right," Lintwo said with a yawn. "Well, good night."

"So what's the principal like?" Sandmera asked.

"More laid back and harder working than I was expecting," Tara said.

"Shouldn't the principal always be hard-working?" Catrin asked.

"With the amount of paperwork she gets, the pace she keeps is intense," Tara replied.

Sandmera stayed up most of the night compiling info on the principal. Her obsession with Mist seemed forgotten. Tara found this just a little out of character for her friend to drop her past obsession so quickly.

The next morning, right after Tara cleaned up and got dressed, Sandmera asked again, "About the principal, anything stand out yet?"

"Well, as you may expect, I think she's really old," Tara said.

"How old, like from before magic reappeared?" Sandmera pressed.

"Maybe?" Tara replied before rushing out. Sandmera had become frantic for info, which was out of character.

10

The Path to an Ending

Class went by in a blur, but instead of looking over paper-work, Lintwo led Tara to a sealed-off engineering area below the workers' quarter. This section had its own dedicated elevator hidden away near the bridge. "I only found out about this area yesterday," Lintwo explained on the way down.

"But didn't you help build our ship?" Tara asked.

"I created the blueprint for it, but some places have been renovated and others added since its launch," Lintwo replied.

The elevator dinged and opened, revealing a worn, water-logged tunnel, its walls rusty with age and dampness. "When was this added?" Tara asked.

"Thirty years ago part of a sewage system was sectioned off for this," Lintwo explained as she led the way deeper into the depicted tunnel, "but I now know a mining craft was recovered and sealed within. We will find out why."

The first half mile was a long line of damp and rusting metal, but after that, more and more lights were in working order and less junk was seen.

Almost a full mile later was a wall sealing off the pipeline. Cameras and automated turrets sat unpowered around the entrance. The vault-like door hung ajar. Lintwo and Tara silently approached the door. After a few seconds of looking around, they slipped inside.

A makeshift hangar greeted them. It had been built at a connecting point to multiple pipe networks. The other pipes were sealed off with flat walls. An old mining ship sat in the center of the room, part of its hold removed. Shattered computers and rusted desks were strewn about. The room felt wrong. The closer to the ship Lintwo went, the stronger the otherworldly feeling became.

"Was this what you were expecting?" Tara asked, clearly oblivious to the feeling of otherworldliness.

The feeling's intensity skyrocketed. Lintwo engulfed the room physically in her magic. The room's stillness echoed in Death. It smelled of shadow and tasted of cold. The otherworldly feeling from the ship retreated. "This is so much worse than I was expecting."

Tara covered herself in her own power. Flames harmlessly engulfed her.

Lintwo closed her eyes and used her aura to poke around the room, trying to zero in on whatever felt so dangerous. Near the mining ship, something tried to latch onto Lintwo's energy. Lintwo pushed a lot of dangerous and unstable raw power into the thing before cutting off her connection to that section of her aura.

The thing detonated. Lintwo did not feel the explosion physically but through her magic as part of it was ripped away.

Lintwo fell to her knees but kept probing the area. To her relief, nothing else unknown stirred. Tara ran over to her friend. "Are you all right?" she asked.

Lintwo wiped her forehead free of sweat. "No, not at all. Whatever that was should not exist." Lintwo hoped she had time to be the hunter and was not already the hunted. Lintwo noted her friend seemed more upset. "I am unharmed, just angry," Lintwo clarified.

Tara helped her friend to her feet and watched as Lintwo began to look over all the shattered devices in the room.

The computers in the room were old now, but new thirty years before. The ship had been partly disassembled by a team that knew what they were doing using proper tools. The serial numbers on the mining ship's parts and its faded markings of A-36 "Spirit of Steel" matched a ship that had gone missing fifty years before. After she was done, Lintwo's magic filled the room once more, but this time the mining craft, tables, chairs, and electronics in the room rotted into dust.

"We are done here," Lintwo spat.

Tara rushed after her very pissed friend. "What exactly happened?"

"I think someone let a force onboard that should have been left well enough alone," Lintwo sighed.

"What, like Death itself?" Tara asked seriously. She, like her ancestors, had been raised to hate World Spirits.

Lintwo gave her friend a long and searching look. "If only all things were so simple," Lintwo sighed before double-timing it back to the school. Tara, who was still shaken, kept her magic tightly wrapped about herself.

The next few weeks were odd. Lintwo spent the first four days looking over the ship studying, then she gave Tara a vacation from helping. On day five Lintwo simply left the dorms and did not contact anyone.

Sandmera stopped obsessing over Lintwo, instead focusing on the old planetary models for their destination. Something about the data seemed to aggravate Sandmera, but when Tara asked about it, Sandmera said her conjecture was self-evident, which other members of the school agreed with regardless of their specialty. Sandmera and Tara drifted apart.

Soon after, others disappeared, mostly miners, maintenance crew, and Sandmera's new growing friend group.

Tara began to keep an eye on some of Sandmera's friends. At a mall Tara noticed one of Sandmera's new friends breaking off from a group, so she followed.

Tara lost track of her quarry near a storage area. A thump sounded behind her. Tara rushed after the noise only to find a very tired-looking Lintwo standing over the collapsed form of their target.

"Another failure," Lintwo muttered, crushing a small squirming orb in her hand not seeming to be very aware of her surroundings.

"What did you do?" Tara asked. Lintwo jolted; her eyes swam to Tara's general direction.

"You are clean and good." Lintwo nodded before turning to leave.

Tara grabbed Lintwo's shoulder and said "Just talk to me." Lintwo collapsed into Tara's arms. "And when was the last time you ate or slept?"

Lintwo pulled out a half-eaten energy bar and tossed it into her mouth. "I just ate," Lintwo said through wild chewing.

"I'm taking you back to the dorms," Tara decided.

"No, too unsafe. Help me walk. I'll give you directions to a safehouse," Lintwo said.

"Then you sleep and tell me what's going on, ok?" Tara said as she helped Lintwo walk.

Lintwo directed her friend through a multitude of side passages and back rooms. After going through a few passages that Tara was sure none of the cleaning crew even knew existed, they arrived at a room with no exit. A brand-new steel plaque reading *1st block, room 1* sat near an old sleeping bag and a pile of flashlights. A footlocker rested near the bag with a disassembled rifle laid on top. The rest of the room was empty; it felt even emptier with the small assortment of gear kept within.

Tara set Lintwo on the sleeping bag. Tara turned around, looking to see if this room really had only one exit. When she turned back, Lintwo held a cup of iced coffee. They shared a long silence, broken only when a dark rippling portal opened next to Lintwo, from which another cup of iced coffee floated out and into Tara's hand.

"It's cold," Tara said.

Lintwo shrugged. "My shadow just can't keep things hot. Do you need sweetener?"

Tara found her friend's nonchalance comforting. One sip was enough to realize the coffee was very bitter. "Yes, please." The portal exerted itself upon reality again, allowing a handful of artificial sugar packets to land in Tara's now ready hands.

When their drinks were finished, Lintwo shook her head clean. "So answers are fine then. I'll say what I can. This goes back to when I was still on the home world. My folks were World Spirits: Death and Water. Don't ask how or why. At some point I was given a task: something had cut off a world from the World Spirits, whose job is to keep things balanced. Like overworked mid-tier administrators, my folks delegated. I was given the task of finding out what happened out here and stopping it. It seems like whatever is causing a mess for my folks found a mining ship from our home first. These things are some kind of parasite that latches onto a host body's mind and soul and slowly puppets them. Some kind of hive mind is at work. I've been caught on the back foot and am trying to slow it down and clean up the ship. The more I learn about this, the more questions I have."

Another long silence began. "That's a lot to take in," Tara said.

Lintwo sighed, rolling her eyes. "Tell me about it. More coffee?"

"Yes, please, no sweetener this time," Tara replied. After taking a sip, she was glad for the bitterness; it kept her new existential dread in check for a little bit longer.

The two friends sat in silence for a long while communing through their memories by staring into their cups.

"So what's our best course of action?" Tara asked.

Lintwo sighed. "I'll cut out the virus infecting our home. You should stay here." She stood up and began to walk.

Tara grabbed her friend's wrist. "What aren't you telling me?"

Lintwo looked into Tara's eyes. "The command crew and many students, medical staff, and technicians are compromised. We are running out of time, Tara. Drastic measures may be required."

"Like what, killing everyone?" Tara demanded. Her friend looked away. "So that's it then?" Tara asked.

"We are running out of time. I'm sorry," Lintwo said as she slipped from Tara's grasp. "In a few hours this should be over," Lintwo said as the shadows in the room swallowed her up.

Lintwo moved through a maze of darkness, separate but connected to the normal physical realm. She hunted down all the things possessing her crew, removing each she found while trying to do as little damage to the humans whose entire being had been hijacked.

Lintwo rushed around. She was getting better at removing the things possessing her crew with less damage to the victims. Some of the older victims, however, were fully taken over, no longer prisoners in their bodies because the hive mind had fully taken over, replacing the body's original inhabitant entirely. For all her power and knowledge, Lintwo was unable to stitch back together something with barely shreds of its former self left.

The school was a nightmare. On one hand, most had not been taken over for very long at all. On the other hand, most of the students were compromised. Lintwo kicked herself mentally. If not for isolating the signature of the thing, she would have fought around the Spirit of Steel.

Lintwo found Sandmera near her office standing with a group of teachers and armed security. Opposing the Sandmera group were some office workers and security huddled behind barricades.

"We just need to find information on where the principal may be," Sandmera said. Her concern could be reasonable, but Lintwo could sense that all of Sandmera's group had been taken over.

"Those doors open for the principal and only the principal," Lintwo's current secretary called over from behind the barricade of furniture. Lintwo made a mental note to try to remember the secretary's name after all this was over.

"We are going through those doors. Don't make us go through you as well," Sandmera said. Weapons were raised on both sides.

Lintwo hopped out of a shadow behind Sandmera's group. "Well, we can't have that."

One of the teachers with Sandmera looked back. "Where have you been, Mist?" Lintwo knew her Mist identity had never even talked with that teacher.

"Am I talking to Sandmera or you?" she asked.

"Both," Sandmera said without turning around. The few ranged weapons had their safeties flipped off.

Lintwo pulled her principal's mask out of a shadow. "Don't go taking over my people. It was hard enough getting their ancestors off the home world." That one piece of truth had not left Lintwo's lips in many lifetimes. It was freeing and helped her focus on what she needed to do. Both sides froze as Lintwo slipped on her helmet and pulled on the shadowy undercurrent all around them, restraining Sandmera's group and pulling the cosmic hitchhikers from their bodies.

Alarms began to go off. Lintwo sensed a surge of movement all around them. A horde was mobilizing. "Inside my office now!" she called out.

"Ma'am?" the secretary asked.

"We have more incoming. Now move!" Lintwo replied as she leapt over the barricade and went through her office door feet first.

The ad hoc defenders rushed into the office. One enterprising guard toppled a bookcase in front of the door. Lintwo skidded to her desk and rapidly began typing on her computer.

The defenders exchanged glances, then shrugged and began piling up more of the principal's very expensive furniture in front of the room's only entry point.

Lintwo activated all the nonlethal traps she could and began shutting off access to all the ship's systems to anyone that was not her. This fail-safe had been put in place for security, anticipating a mutiny, even though Lintwo had never dreamed this would be where her life would lead.

"What are your orders?" a guard called over.

"Try to incapacitate, but don't let anyone get close. An alien parasite took over some of the crew," Lintwo said.

"That sounds far-fetched," another guard said.

Lintwo groaned and then took off her mask, not even trying to hide her anger and annoyance. The shadows around them bubbled. "Tell me, is that any more far-fetched than there still being two crew on those ships that are from the home world? How about after this is over I share some embarrassing stories from Qilpee's childhood?"

"Are you really the principal?" the stubborn guard asked.

"Look, I can't mind-control you like the parasites, but question me again and I will toss you into space," Lintwo snapped.

The stubborn guard raised his gun at Lintwo. Half a second later, the man fell through a shadowy portal at his feet and was deposited outside the ship as it sped onward in the void, leaving him to quickly die from lack of air before he even knew what was happening. Even though the man's finger twitched on his gun's trigger, it would not fire in the vacuum of space.

Lintwo looked at her allies. "Anyone else?" The defenders snapped back to watching the doorway.

Lintwo noticed many attempts at taking over the ship's systems as she overrode each one and took more and more of the system for her own. Lintwo was glad she had been paranoid enough to make sure every major system was built from the ground up to obey her over all else and that she had made sure to keep it that way. Even after all the repairs and replacements, she still had control.

A trap activated within earshot of one of the electrified floors, and then a dummy fire extinguisher spat tear gas. Laser fences hidden in pillars behind a thin layer of plaster sputtered to life, more floors crackled to life, and mists of noxious gas filled the floor.

Lintwo slammed on her mask and tossed some gas masks over to her allies. "They are coming. Don't risk your life. Don't let them get close."

A wall of people marched towards the barricade in lock-step, their eyes glazed over and some still crying.

Lintwo set up a sniper rifle on her desk. Her allies fired at leg height. One by one the horde fell, but their fellows stepped over the fallen in silence. Those that fell coordinated with their horde-mates to make the advance smoother than it had any right to be.

Lintwo lost track of time, switching from one target to another as steady and unfeeling as a good clockwork watch. A bulkhead behind the horde collapsed, falling on a sizable chunk of the possessed crew.

A monstrous roar echoed throughout the ship, overlapping with the sounds of devastation echoing in Lintwo's and the company's ears.

Dust and shards of metal exploded on the horde, obscuring the kill zone, but Lintwo felt most of the horde die in an instant. All those she had tried to save were gone.

Lintwo set up a barrier around her office, the walls and the doorway keeping her own team alive. Shrapnel and dust were consumed by the barrier. "Hold fire!" Lintwo called out, knowing their own fire would also be eaten by the barrier.

The debris cloud glowed. "Shit!" Lintwo swore, recognizing dragon-fire at a glance. Lintwo opened portals under the feet of her team and relocated them to her safehouse.

Lintwo did not have time to relocate herself but managed to dart out of the room as the dragon breath cut through a few decks and the ship lurched.

An immense red dragon's head gazed down at Lintwo. "So they got you too, Qilpee," Lintwo sighed.

Lintwo dusted herself off as she stared into one of Qilpee's huge eyes. Her friend's true form was enormous, fitting for an ancient dragon. *If Qilpee was ancient now and they had known each other from childhood, what did that make Lintwo?* She smirked at the thought, hoping her draconic friend still had some free will left.

Qilpee's head slithered out of the room and Lintwo jumped after her.

Fork in the Road

Lintwo fell into a flaming tunnel dug through her ship. Heat rose as she fell. Lintwo quickly surpassed thermal velocity, but Qilpee was faster. Lintwo caught glimpses of the dragon's flaming breath slagging other parts of the ship and a few scales of its tail. Lintwo had to use the deep shadows cast by the fire to slip through a new hole cut in the tunnel that Qilpee was digging through their home. The only saving grace was they still had an air supply, even if the fire was eating that up quickly.

Lintwo spotted Qilpee's tail slip around a sharp corner. Using her portals, Lintwo slingshotted herself around the turn and flew into the ship's engine room.

Lintwo felt overwhelming heat. She fell into a lengthening shadow and rolled on the floor. Dragon breath collapsed the wall directly behind where Lintwo had been.

Qilpee's tail spun, lashing out; a trail of fire followed. Lintwo jumped to her feet and onto the tail.

Running up the tail of an ancient red dragon who had once been her friend in a fight to the death was not where Lintwo thought her week was going to go.

Lintwo pulled out her knife, tossing it into Qilpee's eye. The dragon's head reeled back, and its fire sputtered out.

Qilpee roared, but Lintwo's knife flew back to her hand. The one gift from Death Lintwo had kept was very good at doing damage to living things.

Lintwo roared. "Qilpee!!!!" Twin roars echoed in her ears.

The dragon's tail arched up and chased after its target. Lintwo's throat was numb, her voice hoarse. Shadows filled the room, pushing back the glowing sun like heat haze produced by dragon fire.

Lintwo neared Qilpee's head, but the glaive-like tail was closing. Lintwo leapt, but the tail did not change course. Lintwo landed on Qilpee's huge dragon head, plunging her knife into it and pushing magic in to disintegrate the brain.

Qilpee's tail impacted her own throat seconds later, ripping it open. "Finally some quiet," Qilpee's voice echoed in the room. "I wish I had been stronger," the dragon said as it died.

Lintwo panted, seeing the last of her old friend's spirit fall apart into nothing.

"You two were better people than I ever was. I'll set things right." Lintwo forced the words out between ragged breaths as she watched her tears fall on the dragon's body.

Looking around, most of the engine's main control room was still working. Lintwo got to work double-checking the scouting logs and ship's course. Slowly she ran many calculations and initiated a process with no going back.

Tara ran. She had encased herself in as much magic as possible, her steps searing into the floor.

Few bodies and fewer people lingered in the halls. It was unnerving to see passageways that had been choked with a crew of thousands for years without end deserted save for the dying, the dead, and the lost.

Echoes of a titanic clash reverberated through the ship's bones and the souls of its occupants. Never before had Tara thought just how vulnerable and small their titanic home was within the universe. A swift death in the void seemed all too likely.

Tara found more dead than dying as she neared the school.

A handful of sprinklers around her (the ones that still had power and were not smashed yet) sputtered to life. Tara skidded to a stop, halting at the only working screen nearby. The ad for a new bar called the Spirited Lion, depicting a lion running around a planet-shaped cork set in a bottle of cheap ale, fizzed out, being replaced with Lintwo's face.

Lintwo sat in a very singed chair at the engine room's master control panel.

The course had been set. All overrides had been locked out. All that was left was a farewell, mostly because Lintwo did not want to leave the descendants of her former foes turned charges to languish in ignorance any longer.

"Most of you know me as the principal. My real name is Lintwo Reaper. I share blood with Lindy and Frost, the Death and Water World Spirits of this reality. A long time ago I designed this ship before our journey began." Lintwo sighed and took off her mask. "Some of you know me as Mist from the maintenance department. I fought in a war against your ancestors. It was a war of genocide they started and lost. I made sure those who were left lived. I did not just do this out of the kindness of my heart or out of sorrow for a dear friend I lost in that war, one I killed with my own hands. Something slipped into this reality, this universe, from the spaces beyond this place. That thing took over parts of this crew fifty years ago, but thanks to data gathered, I know its exact coordinates. I don't need any of you anymore. This ship is set to split apart. I'm taking the main engines with me. The rest will be sent on a new trajectory to a system with a number of worlds with thick atmospheres and gravity close to the home world's. With some time and teamwork, those worlds could be terraformed into good homes for your descendants. I wish you all good luck, and, oh, my newest aide will be getting all my access permissions an hour after the ships separate."

When on their way, the ship split into two halves, one spinning off towards the best safe harbor in the surrounding systems, the other towards an ending of something. The engine block and the bulk of the ship's generators were locked in on a collision course to the asteroid that had corrupted her ship.

Lintwo leaned back and got lost in her memories of the past as reverberations of the ship shuddered around her. Years passed as she slumbered.

The engine block began to shake violently. Lintwo opened her eyes and checked the exterior cameras. A huge hole in space and time filled the screen. One eye, larger than many suns, peered through the hole in reality. "So much for wanting to live forever," Lintwo chuckled.

Lintwo spared one last glance at Qilpee's still cooling body before accelerating the ship even more and setting the generators to detonate.

The eye before her widened seconds before the engine block impacted. Fire and raw, unchained magic filled the control room. Lintwo felt her body begin to melt. She cackled, feeling free for the first time since her birth.

Qilpee's voice echoed in Lintwo's dying mind. "Live." Samandrea's voice echoed, "Live." One by one, voices of everyone she had met echoed, "Live." Faces of the dead, those she had killed, met in passing, or worked closely with, all flashed past.

"Don't ask for that, anything but that!" Lintwo cried out. It felt like the dead were dogging her heels, and that made the despair and regrets worse.

Sandmera's voice echoed, "You were always there for us. Please live." The voices of the dead echoed in assent.

"I'll be back," Lintwo yelled into the abyss, her voice drowned out to a whisper by the searing pain. Overwhelming sounds of burning and, above all, devastation echoed the cries of a mortally wounded eldritch horror from between realities. Lintwo covered herself in as many barriers as possible and used the last of her energy to summon ice all around her. Her ride slipped past the veil of the only reality Lintwo had ever known.

Lintwo opened her eyes and frantically checked herself over. She was whole. One camera, once set in a hallway, now peered out into the void. A verdant green world loomed in its blurry vision. "Son of a bitch, next time I see a Fate, we are having words."

But that is a story for another time, from another place.

Evan A. Cushing lives in Salem, Massachusetts.